Maureen Murphy Williams

CATAPULT

A Mo the Shelter Cat
Mystery

Catapult
A Mo the Shelter Cat Mystery
All Rights Reserved
Copyright @2017 Maureen Murphy Williams

Cover Photo @2017 Gordon Gutchess. All rights reserved – used with permission.

Catmandu Books

ISBN: 0692883428

ACKNOWLEDGMENTS

Since each of us is blessed with only one life, why not live it with a cat? *Robert Stearns*

Morgan (Mo), the inspiration for this cat detective series, was a longtime shelter resident. Much of her three-year stay in shelters was spent at the Cat Adoption Team in Sherwood, Oregon. The patience and love shown by staff in shelters everywhere, and especially at CAT, are only a few of the reasons cats in shelters can thrive, and so many are placed in loving homes.

CAT and I hope Morgan's story will inspire more people to help a shelter animal. A portion of the *Mo the Shelter Cat Mystery* series book sales is pledged to CAT for all they do. You can check CAT out at: www.catadoptionteam.org.

MO

IMPORTANT FELINE CHARACTERS

MO

A beautiful gray and white feline whose proper name is Morgan, came to the shelter when her 'mum' was murdered. Our feline heroine, Mo is companion to Kate Ferguson and Ambassador to Cats Pause Feline Shelter. Mo also serves as the Winery Cat for Kats Jory Hills Estate Vineyard and Winery, a duty she takes seriously even though grapes are not her favorite indulgences.

MONA, MAC and MURPHY

A former feral Tiger mom and her two Maine Coon offspring, these kitties were adopted and are adored by Yamhill County Commissioner George King. Although sleuths by nature, these three have their hands full with George, who always manages to find himself in the center of trouble in Seven Oaks, Oregon.

LADY and *SEÑOR*

Two feral cats rescued by Olivia Knightly, they now enjoy a world of barn moussing and home life with Olivia at Andrew Knightly's horse ranch and vineyard.

WINSTON and SQUEAKER

Two shelter cats adopted by Olivia Knightly to join *LADY* and *SEÑOR* at the Knightly Ranch, where they collude with their fellow felines in the arts of moussing and human-keeping.

GEORGIA

A beautiful midnight black feline who found her purr-fect family with Rebecca Sherlock and Rebecca's new baby, Lawrence Junior. Georgia and Mo were instrumental in discovering Lawrence Senior's murderer in Seven Oaks, Oregon.

ANDREW and *SARAH*, aka *ARBOR* and *SYRAH*

Nick-named as a tribute to vineyards everywhere, these two "belong" to veterinarian, James Middleton, and are James' veterinary clinic greeters, where they exude relaxation and contentment to stressed feline clinic patients.

DIANA and *EDWARD*

A beautiful Siamese and a handsome Tuxedo cat respectively, they are a lovely pair who reside with the Kensingtons and their daughters, Pippa and Beatrice. This genteel human family arranges kitty play dates with *PHILLIP*, a dashing gray, brown and black Maine Coon with only one seeing eye, now in his furr-ever home with Elizabeth Conley.

VICTORIA

A black kitten rescued from the back of a delivery truck by *LADY and SEÑOR* at the Knightly Ranch, now residing with Elizabeth Conley and *PHILLIP*.

iii

IMPORTANT HUMAN CHARACTERS

Kate Ferguson

Director of Cats Pause Feline Shelter and champion for felines in and around Seven Oaks, Oregon, Kate is the proud adopted 'mum' to *MO*. Kate is also proprietor of Kats English Bed and Breakfast, her lifelong dream, which is located on her father's property, Kats Jory Hills Estate Vineyard and Winery.

Lt. Charles Beltz

Community Services Coordinator, Yamhill County police department detective. Friend (and more) to Kate.

James Middleton

Local veterinarian, proprietor of The Cats Meow Clinic. Da' to *ARBOR* and *SYRAH*.

Mary Malone

James' veterinarian's assistant (and more?) at The Cats Meow Clinic, Kate's best friend.

John Ferguson

Kate's father and owner of Kats Jory Hills Estate Vineyard and Winery.

Olivia Knightly

Volunteer at Cats Pause, mum to *LADY* and *SEÑOR*, and to *WINSTON* and *SQUEAKER*, daughter of Andrew Knightly.

Andrew Knightly

Olivia's father, owner of The Knightly Ranch, Andrew raises champion Tennessee Walking Horses and keeps a small vineyard.

George King

Editor of the *Jory Hills Times*, a Yamhill County Commissioner, George is da' to *MONA*, *MAC* and *MURPHY*.

Rebecca Sherlock

Owner of the gathering and reunion business, "Let's Get Together." Widow of Lawrence Senior and 'Mum' to *GEORGIA* and new arrival, Lawrence Junior.

Elizabeth Conley

Proprietress of the burgeoning business, The Print Shoppe. Purr-fect match for *PHILLIP*, her adopted lifetime feline companion. New mum to *VICTORIA*, who is also now companion to *PHILLIP*.

Michael Middleton

James' younger brother, a skilled horse trainer.
Newly-minted entrepreneur whose idea for
single-serving premium wine sales is backed by
a mysterious Japanese millionaire former stock
trader.

William Kent

Kats Jory Hills Estate winemaker. Lobbyist for
vineyards and wineries in the Jory Hills
American Viticultural Area (AVA).

The Kensingtons

A lovely English couple, with daughters,
Beatrice and Pippa. Purr-fect matches to
DIANA and *EDWARD.*

Gerald Hawking

A local farmer who hosts Halloween festivities
in his pumpkin patch, featuring a pumpkin toss,
corn mazes, hay rides and a pumpkin catapult.

Sun Yuen Wong

Manager of a group of Japanese wine salesmen who visited Yamhill County wineries with the intention of importing premium Oregon wines to Japan for Chan Wine Distributors.

Chen Wu

Former Japanese stockbroker, now a consultant to Japanese corporations specializing in mergers and acquisitions.

Welcome to My World!

Mo

x

CATAPULT

CHAPTER 1 –

There's no need for a piece of sculpture in a home that has a cat. *Wesley Bates*

As darkness descended over the pumpkin patch, the three cats stared into the field with intense concentration. There was something in the field that wasn't a pumpkin, something that didn't belong there. Slowly and on their bellies, the cats crept into the damp pumpkin vines, a path that allowed them to skirt around the cornfield, moving as quietly as the mice they often hunted in this field.

They closed in on the object in their sights and suddenly stopped in their tracks, tails bottle-brushed and backs arched.

What is that THING? demanded the big gray and white cat, the leader of the pack. *I've never seen anything like it, and I hope it isn't ALIVE!*

The three cats crawled toward the huge dark object that had so frightened them. It

1

didn't move, but that didn't mean it *couldn't* move...

The giant object was a catapult, a scary addition to the field, but inert and harmless. The farmer had moved the giant into the field earlier that day – before the cats descended upon the field for their nightly hunt.

In this small corn and pumpkin farm, farmer Gerald Hawking relied upon burgeoning seasonal agritourism to provide 30 percent of his income. Although he had not yet begun to offer nighttime activities, the daytime festivities began in late September and would continue through Halloween. Preparations for the events had begun in the spring, when the corn maze was planted, and continued through the late summer and early fall when the costumes for employees arrived, the barn was enhanced and converted to a haunted house, and the macabre embellishments were completed. This short season involved a lot of concentrated activity which would culminate on Halloween. For, the farmer would sigh, "after Halloween a pumpkin's just a pumpkin."

In addition to the thrill of sending a pumpkin to its demise via the giant catapult, visitors could purchase tickets for the zombie paintball hayride, the no-fright Pumpkinland corn maze which included face painting and pumpkin cookie-making, the Nightmare on Sumac Street Haunted House which completely took over the farmer's giant hay barn, and a concession offering pumpkin ice cream atop warm pumpkin pie along with ears of steaming corn on the cob skewered onto sticks.

Now though, the catapult and the dark corn and pumpkin fields were covered with a thin layer of fog on this cold clear night, adding to the eeriness of the scene.

As the cats moved cautiously forward toward the now-demystified catapult, the air was suddenly filled with the scent of something else — human death. The cats abandoned caution and raced around the behemoth, only to stop short again at the sight they encountered.

For what they saw, the cats doubted the farmer had intended.

A human scarecrow stood guard in front of the catapult. Not that the scarecrow was a living human any longer.

As they gazed up at the hideous sight, the cats gagged and spat trying to rid themselves of the smell of death and decaying human flesh. A useless task because the scarecrow wasn't going anywhere. It stared down at them with sightless eyes, a floppy hat covering its head and straw stuffed into the sleeves of its old coat.

The cats knew there was nothing they could do for this human. Dead is dead. But they had to let their own humans know what they'd found. They did not recognize the scent of the dead man, and for that they were grateful. But somewhere, someone would be missing this poor soul. Selfishly, they were glad this lonely guardian of the silent field wasn't one of their own precious humans.

CATAPULT

CHAPTER 2 -

The cat is domestic only as far as suits its own ends… Saki (H.H. Munro)

Kate Ferguson and Mary Malone were settling in to enjoy a late evening cup of tea in the great room parlour of Kate's bed-and-breakfast establishment, Kats English B&B.

Kate had realized her dream when she began to visualize – and then complete – her B&B the previous year. Situated in the lovely former carriage house at her father's vineyard property, Kate had toiled relentlessly to build something special.

Kats English B&B was distinguished from other lodgings in the surrounding wine country by a considerable number of modern comforts and special amenities.

The six suites offered feather beds, down pillows and comforters, as well as in-suite loos with spa tubs. Heating and air conditioning invited guests year-round to comfort and privacy, along with the provision of luxurious robes and linens, I-Pod docks and Wi-Fi.

The B&B common areas included a library, comfortably furnished for reading and playing cards and games. An inviting sunroom beckoned guests to enjoy morning coffee or tea, or they could sip the brews family-style with other guests in the separate dining room, followed by a hearty English breakfast. Tea was offered each afternoon, served with warm fresh-baked scones with jam and clotted cream.

With the colder nights approaching, warming by the great room's giant lava stone fireplace was an event to covet.

Kate was currently hosting the top five wine salesmen and their manager from Chan Wine Distributors of Japan for an overnight stay before they caught a mid-morning flight the next day to Santiago, Chile. Kats English B&B had thrilled the Japanese visitors with its local charm and proximity to not only beautiful vineyards, lush gardens and koi ponds, but a top local winery as well.

"We have a very small window of time to allow our Japanese visitors to know us as farmers and family," Kate told Mary. "Dad and William Kent took them to see the bottling room with its new screw-top equipment, barrel and keg rooms, and of course, the tasting facility. This is the first time we've hosted wine connoisseurs from outside the United States. As you know, Dad's wine is currently sold in fifteen states.

"Chan Company has said that Japan Airlines wants three pallets of premium Pinot Noir. That's 69 cases of wine, and it likely won't last JAL a month if served continuously."

Kate suddenly cocked her head and stood up.

"Wouldn't you know it? Just when I begin to feel relaxed and calm, I get that same odd feeling something isn't right with Mo and her friends. Have you seen her in the last hour? You know, she's been visiting the field next door nightly with Phillip and Victoria. Those two cats have been staying with us while Elizabeth Conley is on vacation. I love them all to pieces, but the three of them are a handful."

"I know you and Mo have, well, a *sensitivity* to each other's thoughts," Mary offered diplomatically as she shook her head ever so slightly, "but I think those three cats together are a formidable force. They have just enjoyed the heck out of their nightly field excursions. Now, they're likely doing just fine, but if they aren't back in the next fifteen minutes, we can certainly go looking for them."

"Oh, thank you for being so thoughtful and understanding, Mary," said Kate as she remained standing wringing her hands. "Those cats mean everything to me, and the cats at the shelter wouldn't know what to do without Mo, their feline hero and placement liaison. I'm so grateful Mo chose me as her human companion."

"That poor girl did have a rough start, didn't she," sighed Mary. "Why, she was nearly catatonic when I first saw her at the shelter after her human was murdered. I'm grateful that 'Charles and Company,' Charles Beltz and the McMinnville Police Department, found the murderer. But I can't help but think that Mo and the other cats had something to do with the speedy apprehension of the killer."

Just then, three agitated cats sprang through the cat door from the outside. All three were whining and shrieking, their hair spiked high and fangs bared. They jumped to the window sill and began howling.

"Good grief you three," exclaimed Kate. "You look like you've seen a ghost, and with

Halloween around the corner, well you may have! What are you looking out at?"

Oh mum, meowed Mo, *something terrible has happened! I'm so glad you and Mary are here safe and sound and warm. But there is a poor soul in the field who isn't so fortunate!*

"So much chatter from you, Mo," said Kate as she rushed toward Mo. "There is obviously something wrong, Mary. I think we should take our jackets and flashlights and venture into the field next door to investigate."

"Very well, but I'm expecting James to stop by for a few minutes," noted Mary. "I'll just give him a call to see where he's at, and let him know we'll be out 'catastrophe-hunting' in farmer Gerald's field. If I didn't know better, I might think you just want to see his new Halloween attractions and get into the mood for the season."

"Mo," admonished Kate, "I want you and Phillip and Victoria to stay with us and not go running off. There will be no lost cats on my watch!"

The cats bounced around each other, flopped on their backs, stood on their hind legs, and continued their mewling and howling until Kate and Mary gave up and covered their ears.

And so, this group of five sleuths prepared to trudge into the night.

CATAPULT

CHAPTER 3 -

You cannot look at a sleeping cat and feel tense. *Jane Pauley*

As Mary began to call James Middleton on her cell phone, through the parlour window both Kate and Mary spotted the 'Spay Station,' The Cats Meow's mobile clinic, winding down the darkened lane toward the carriage house B&B. The Spay Station – a sight it was – had been lovingly painted with pictures of neon cats in space suits, while planets, stars and galaxies swirled around them.

James literally jumped from the van, with his two charges, Arbor and Syrah on his heels.

CATAPULT

Arbor

Syrah

The bonded pair was formerly named
Andrew and Sarah for the English royals, but

after he adopted the abandoned duo, James renamed them as a tribute to the local vineyards.

Although James was a veterinarian and was careful in the transporting of all the cats in his care, both Arbor and Syrah put up such a racket when 'caged' in their carriers, that he usually allowed them to ride in the carpeted and protected area of the van where they could see out the windows. They were safe there because the van had padded walls on three sides. He called their van riding area, "The Throne Room," and the cats knew immediately where to go when the van door opened for a potential ride. If the van was going a long distance to assist a feline in need, James would tell the cats, 'nope, long trip,' and they knew they had to accept the stay of safety in their home or at his clinic. Too much riding made the cats a bit car sick. James – and the cats – had found that out the hard way.

"Good evening, ladies," James greeted the two women friends as he reached the door. "You have your jackets on – are you going out somewhere?"

Mary stifled a giggle, and said to James, "We're headed to the field next door to see what has so disturbed the cats. They came roaring through the cat door just a few minutes ago, and they seemed quite agitated. I was just dialing you up to let you know where we would be."

CATAPULT

"Well, let's just add me and my two to this melee and see where it takes us," quipped James. "I hope your Japanese guests have not been disturbed by all of this."

"I don't believe so," said Kate in a hushed voice. "They're ensconced in their rooms at the rear of the B&B and it's very quiet there. We should, though, keep our voices down outside."

James, Mary and Kate, flashlights in hands, and the five cats started the trek from the B&B to the pumpkin patch. It was a crisp fall evening, and the skies were clear and the moon glowed with a harvest hue. The trail took them through a stand of fir trees that jutted majestically between the carriage house B&B, a smaller single-clone vineyard on the Kats Jory Hills Estate property, and the pumpkin patch. The woods were dark but smelled fresh and luscious. The scent of pine made them all quite heady as they made their way to the field.

As the hybrid group reached the edge of the pumpkin patch, the moon shone on the catapult, making it look like a giant oil well bathed in a pale greenish-yellow glow.

At that moment, all five cats started howling. The noise jolted the small band of humans and the cats darted ahead around the catapult to the dark form propped upright on poles near several stacked bales of hay.

CATAPULT

"Good Lord!" exclaimed Mary as she followed the cats, rounded the catapult and took in the sight. "What in the world is that?"

The three focused their flashlights on the specter that now revealed itself to be a human form dressed as a scarecrow.

"I don't believe my eyes," cried Kate. "How dreadful! I'm dialing the police right now, and we should stand well away from whatever that is – or was – until they get here. I do hope Charles is at the department because if not, I'll be calling him at home!"

CATAPULT

CHAPTER 4 -

One must love a cat on its own terms. *Paul Gray*

Given the hour and the darkness that enveloped them, the cats were wired as if they'd inhaled coffee or some other stimulant. Cats are naturally nocturnal and not one of these five was ready to leave the field until the police arrived and they could glean some information about the 'scarecrow.'

Morgan, a ten-year-old gray and white girl with spider-web-like markings on her flank, was sensitive to remarks about her size. Mo was a large cat, but upon hearing any discussion regarding her weight, she would simply hiss, *I'm big-boned with excellent muscle tone.* She had beautiful green eyes and an extremely expressive countenance, especially when tormented – or bored.

CATAPULT

Mo

       Phillip and Victoria were companions to Elizabeth Conley. Phillip was a mostly-Maine Coon feline who had but one seeing eye, thanks to a stick-wielding youngster. The accident happened when he was a kitten, but the impairment didn't slow him down one bit. Phillip had met Morgan at Cats Pause while awaiting his furr-ever home. He and Elizabeth proved to be devoted to each other upon first meeting, and finding they couldn't live without each other, Phillip left the shelter to be with Elizabeth forever.

Phillip

Victoria was found by felines Lady and Señor at the Knightly Ranch one day as she hid in the back of a delivery truck. Because she had no claws, Olivia Knightly relegated Victoria to staying inside while the other cats moussed around in the barns and cavorted with the horses. To resolve that dilemma, Elizabeth brought Victoria occasionally to her home to keep Phillip company, as he too was lonely for feline companionship. The two cats were now as bonded as siblings, and would remain together with Elizabeth.

Victoria

As the cats circled the human group, they were anxious to stay close and hear what had happened, but at the same time, they were spooked and wanted to flee as far from the pumpkin patch as possible.

The humans stood well back from the scarecrow out of respect for both the dead man and the integrity of the crime scene. For how could it be anything other than a crime?

Minutes later and at the sound of approaching sirens, cats and humans began to carefully back away further from the gruesome sight to the perimeter of the field. They wished to leave plenty of room for the arriving police and the crime scene investigators to do their jobs.

Someone in law enforcement must have given the go-ahead signal, because suddenly the entire field was filled with bright light from spotlights, and with police and fire personnel, crime scene investigators, crime scene photographers and of course, the medical examiner.

Lt. Charles Beltz had been first to arrive, but after spotting Kate and Company standing at a safe distance, waited next to his car for back-up. Born and raised in Salem, Oregon, Charles had attended Linfield College in McMinnville on a baseball scholarship. During his junior year, he tore his anterior cruciate ligament and decided that he couldn't make a living playing baseball. He decided to give up the game, and transferred to Western Oregon University where he majored in police science. Currently the Community Coordinator with Yamhill County, Charles was the liaison between city, county and state police. Tall, with broad shoulders and thick brown military-style hair and laughing eyes, Charles preferred reading and horseback riding in his spare time. That is, until he met Kate. A bit older than Kate, Charles was nearing his mid-thirties, and longed for a true companion. He had immediately arrived at the conclusion that Kate was perfect for him.

CATAPULT

Kate Ferguson, with her shoulder length coppery auburn hair and classic features, sported jaunty freckles and lovely cat-like green eyes. Kate's tiny frame belied her knack for complete command of Cats Pause Feline Shelter and she was devoted to its mission. A transplant from Roanoke, Virginia, she had attended Oregon State University, where she'd majored in agriculture and viticulture, and minored in veterinary medicine. There, Kate met Brian whom she'd planned to marry, and later lost him to a roadside explosion in Afghanistan. Kate also lost her mother, the beautiful Kat Ferguson to cancer around that time, and her childhood home had burned to the ground leaving her without roots. Living in the carriage house on her transplanted father's Oregon vineyard, Kate eventually turned the house into a B&B of extraordinary design. As the proud director of Cats Pause Feline Shelter, she had helped hundreds of felines successfully find their furr-ever homes. She and Charles had developed a loving relationship, and were now comfortable with each other and their respective roles in Seven Oaks.

James Middleton was passionate about animals, and cats were his specialty. Athletic and intelligent, he was blessed with electric blue eyes, dark hair and a fit torso. Although he had been married and divorced in his youth, James had matured and longed to be a family man. But he'd decided after his disastrous marriage he must be content to be da' to Arbor and Syrah for a good while.

Then he'd met raven-haired Mary Malone, with her sharp intelligence and sparkling blue eyes. Mary had devoted her time to animals as well, and had attended a Salem community college where she'd enrolled in biology and pre-med studies, and had graduated as a veterinary technician. She then worked in several Salem veterinary clinics where she honed her skills and developed a passion for animals. When she applied to be James' veterinarian's assistant in Wine Country, James snapped her up and never regretted the decision. As James grew to know Mary better, he became enamored with the willowy brunette, and now divided his time between the practice, his cats, and Mary Malone.

"I regret that you'll all have to stay around the pumpkin patch a short while to be interviewed," said Charles as he walked toward the group while buttoning his police jacket to the chill. "Do you know if there are any other witnesses?"

"Not that we know of," replied Kate. "The cats actually alerted us to something amiss in the field. We trudged out here with our flashlights, but you are seeing exactly what we saw. There was no one else around when we arrived."

"Thank you, Kate," smiled Charles. "After the detectives interview you — and I promise it won't take very long in this cold – I'll finish what I can here and meet all of you at the B&B where it's warm, and we can discuss anything else that may cross your minds by then. Bizarre scene, to say the least. When did the field-owner bring in the catapult?"

Mary looked around and replied, "We think he just moved it in late today. I certainly didn't notice it this morning and I wouldn't have missed something that large – and, well unique – in his pumpkin patch."

"No doubt," said Charles as he surveyed the scene. "Would you mind taking the cats with you when you leave? They look like they're ready to jump out of their skins, and I don't want any of the crime scene techs to accidentally step on a tail or suffer an accidental clawing for doing it."

The cats had already begun their move from the field to the woods, and were ready to make a beeline for the safety of Kate's B&B and a warm fire.

Last one to the carriage house is a rotten pumpkin! squealed Morgan as the cats tore through the night.

"Don't worry, Charles," replied Kate as she and Mary awaited further interviews, "those guys are way ahead of us, and will beat us back to the house by a long shot!"

CATAPULT

CHAPTER 5 -

Dogs come when they are called; cats take a message and get back to you later. Mary Bly

Having completed the preliminary interview process in the field, Mary, James and Kate made their way back to Kat's B&B, and to the warmth it offered. Beckoning them to the house were a crackling fire in the fireplace where five cats sprawled on the hearth, and the promise of hot cider that Kate had brewed earlier in the day.

"I simply do not understand how a township as small as Seven Oaks attracts such chaos," mourned Kate. "Why, we've had three murders here just in the past two years, and now perhaps, a fourth."

As Mary served up Kate's seasonal hot cider, she also gave the cats some lovely chopped chicken breast that Kate had purchased at the grocery earlier that day. Kate directed Mary to the cupboard where a stash of home-baked pumpkin cookies also awaited consumption.

James sat in a padded wicker chair and enjoyed being waited on. Living alone, he didn't get much pampering, and when Mary decided to take charge, he knew better than to – nor did he want to – interfere.

"I agree with you, Kate, and for the life of me, I don't know why these villainous types find Oregon Wine Country so appealing. There are plenty of opportunities for them in the bigger cities. Mary, you don't have to wait on me you know, but if you insist, I really appreciate it."

The three sat around a large round coffee table facing the fireplace. The contrast between the warm safe room and the cold desolate field was very stark. They couldn't help but discuss what they had seen, yet they were reticent to talk about the tragic event.

"I didn't recognize the dead man," ventured Mary. "Not that I got that close to see, much less study, his face – if a face was under that hat at all. Why kill someone and prop him in a field like a scarecrow? It's most certainly not a lethal Halloween prank, nor can I glean any kind of message from the masquerade."

"Mary, I hope you'll sleep tonight," replied James as he savoured his cider and pumpkin cookies. "I, for one, may have difficulty in that respect. If you do find yourself thrashing about, please give me a call and we can talk each other down from the ceiling. Your voice is so soothing; I see the effect it has on the cats every day. They just love to be around you."

"I may have to take you up on that offer, James," sighed Mary as she wiped cookie crumbs on her apron. "That was a gruesome sight I won't soon forget, and talking about other things, anything else, usually helps me calm down."

"I wonder if Charles has found anything that would answer some of the questions in this bizarre death," wondered James out loud. "You know, he may be a while out there. It's got to be a difficult task directing all those investigators in the dark. And knowing Charles, he will want to be a hands-on investigator in this one."

"No doubt at all," sighed Kate, as she, too, wrestled with cookie crumbs. "He is so devoted to his work. I don't know how he finds time for anything else, yet he does, I'm happy to say. Did you know that his cookbook, *The Compleat Jory Hills Wine Country Cuisine/Wine Pairing Journal* is on Powell's local author bestseller list? You know he took all kinds of grief from his police buddies for publishing a cookbook. But Charles is one to follow his heart, no matter what anyone else might say."

The five cats lay in a circle before the fire, their tails curled protectively around their bodies. All five wondered too, how humans could perpetrate such heinous crimes and they felt very fortunate to have found normal, loving homes with kind humans. They too, would find it difficult to erase the image of the dead man dressed as a scarecrow they had witnessed that night.

It promised to be a very long night in Seven Oaks, Oregon.

CATAPULT

CHAPTER 6 -

Cats are the ultimate narcissists. You can tell this by all the time they spend on personal grooming. Dogs aren't like this. A dog's idea of personal grooming is to roll in a dead fish. *James Gorman*

Charles made his way to Kate's B&B after several hours of gathering gruesome details and directing the investigation at the scene.

Just before he reached the driveway to the carriage house, Kate's father, John Ferguson hailed him from the porch of his house next door.

"Charles!" shouted John. "Have you news about the "scarecrow death" yet? I talked to Kate earlier but didn't want to get in your way out in the field. I also called Gerald Hawking, the owner of the corn farm and pumpkin patch. I assume you had a chance to interview him?"

CATAPULT

"Good evening, John," replied Charles. "Not the best of circumstances, but I'm glad to see you. Yes, I did speak with Mr. Hawking. He told me he'd just completed the set-up of the Halloween décor in the pumpkin patch late this afternoon. He left the field before dinner, and there had been no scarecrow – or human – anywhere near the catapult at that time. He did mention that there was a scarecrow in the distant cornfield, but it was a familiar figure, one he had dressed and placed there several weeks earlier. It appears that some of the accoutrements for this macabre scene were 'borrowed' from that other scarecrow."

"Atrocious, this stuff," said John. "Kate is quite upset, and I don't blame her, having seen the human scarecrow with her own eyes. Do you think the crime happened here – or was the body moved to the field after he was killed? So many questions, so few answers."

"We don't know much of anything yet, John," stated Charles as he began removing his gloves. "The lack of blood at the scene might suggest he was killed somewhere else, but at this stage it's impossible to say for sure, but then he did not appear to have any bloody wounds. We'll resume our search tomorrow morning and we have the area cordoned off. I told Mr. Hawking that his pumpkin patch will be a crime scene for at least the next few days."

"Thank you for your scrutiny, Charles," said John. "We all feel safer with you around. I'll let you go inside and warm up. Autumn has certainly arrived after our very warm summer. I'm glad we've completed the grape harvest and it promises to be a record year for our crops."

Charles removed his mud-caked boots at the side door to the B&B, and left them outside along with his gloves. He knew there were only the Japanese men staying there this evening. He was glad there weren't more tourists to worry about, and as he opened the door with a polite tapping on the knocker, he hung his damp coat in the hallway.

"Charles, please come in and warm yourself by the fire," invited Kate. "I know you'll probably need to return to the station soon, but first, take the chill off and have some hot cider," offered Kate as she rushed to the kitchen to prepare a steaming mug for Charles.

"I do really appreciate it, Kate," said Charles as his frame filled the vacant chair around the table, closest to the fireplace. "I don't have much to report, as it is most difficult to find clues in the dark, but at least we've gotten a start and have some of the facts sorted out regarding the condition of the field and the timing of the crime.

"By the way, Kate, I ran into your father on the way here. He was a big help to us as he got the farm owner over here immediately so we could interview him and establish some timeframes."

"Dad wanted to help," Kate called from the kitchen, "but he didn't want to be in the way. I'm glad he could offer some assistance."

"I'm going to wait until morning to interview your guests, Kate," said Charles. "I understand they have a meeting set with Mike Middleton tomorrow, so they'll be up early. I'm sort of surprised Mike hasn't shown up here tonight, James, if only to beg for some of this hot cider."

"I tried calling my brother," offered James, "but have been unable to reach him. He was supposed to be meeting with some vintners earlier today somewhere near here. I wanted to ask if he had seen or heard anything unusual in the area. It's odd he doesn't answer his cell phone, but maybe he's either out of range or he's turned the darned thing off."

"Well, I'm sure he's busy with his project," said Charles. "But if and when you are able to reach him, I'd appreciate if you would ask if he has any information about what went on here today.

"I will take another mug of this cider, if you don't mind, Kate, but then I need to be on my way. I'm sorry you are right on top of the crime scene, and that you all had to be the ones to discover the body. You know, of course, that I'll need all of you to stop by the station tomorrow to make formal statements."

"We're happy to help," said James, "and you can count on our testimonies for the record. Mary, I can stop by to pick you up in the morning, if you like."

"That would be great, James," said Mary. "I will be staying here tonight to keep Kate and the cats company, and I'll help out with breakfast for the guests so that Kate can go to the shelter early to tend to new arrivals."

The cats stood in unison, and stretched and yawned. The fire was so welcoming, but they were anxious to continue their sleuthing in the morning. The human group broke up and the cats, minus James' two felines, lay down again before the fire.

There's nothing we can do tonight, yawned Mo. *We'll sneak back to the field at first light. Well, maybe we should wait for Mary to give us a big breakfast to sustain us. Investigating can be strenuous work.*

CATAPULT

CHAPTER 7 -

Cats do not have to be shown how to have a good time, for they are unfailingly ingenious in that respect. *James Mason*

Later that evening, James returned to the Cats Meow Clinic before driving to his home for bed rest. James was feeling jittery after the events that had occurred next to Kat's Jory Hills Vineyard, and especially since Mary was right in the middle of the murder investigation, too.

After checking on the cats that were staying overnight in the clinic, he discovered that a message awaited him on the clinic's answering service. The message was from Mike. While he listened, he grew wary of the tone of his brother's message. James knew he could have been easily reached by cell phone, so this call appeared to be an attempt to avoid person-to-person conversation.

"Bro," the message began, *"I'm sorry to rush away like this with no notice, but my investor stopped by early this evening and asked if I could make a quick trip to California with him in a company jet to discuss the completion of the single-serving wines contract. If this meeting goes well, we may have the opportunity to produce our own, single-serving bottled wines within a few months. As you know, I've contacted Kate's father about buying some of his premium wine, and hope we can find other vineyards that are interested in a commitment to this project. I'll give you a call when I'm headed back this way. Take it easy, bro."*

Mike had not previously mentioned a rush to complete the single-serving project. James was slightly annoyed that Mike hadn't confided in him, but he was more concerned that perhaps Mike had not done so because there was something 'off' about the deal. None of this sounded like his brother, especially 'jetting' off on a whim. Although it might be his imagination, even Mike's voice had seemed strained, like he was not feeling as confident about the venture as he was attempting to convince James he was.

James and Mike had not always been close friends as siblings.

James had gone to college in Corvallis, and had been a talented baseball player. He had not taken his studies seriously because he loved the game so much. He also loved the ladies, and became known as an adept player, both on and off the field. Then James met Sally, and he decided he'd had enough games. He enrolled in OSU's school of veterinary medicine, and he and Sally were married within three months. James loved Sally, but he became so obsessed with animal medicine that he began paying less and less attention to her. Sally had been a cheerleader in college, and she wasn't used to being ignored. She soon became bored and sought attention with other men. James' marriage ended as it had begun: in a flash.

But James was less devastated by Sally's departure and the failure of his marriage than he was with the predicaments his younger brother Mike had a habit of getting into. Mike had always felt that since he couldn't walk in James' footsteps, he would make every deliberate attempt to walk the other way. Certainly, James had not meant for him to feel that way. They were simply two entirely different personalities.

While James had excelled in sports and was admired by women, Mike was not much interested in sports nor did women find him particularly charismatic. He was dark and handsome with the same blue eyes as James, but Mike followed the horses – and he started betting heavily on the races. At first, he followed them because it was entertainment. Then it became clear that Mike had a gambling addiction. More than once, James had come to

CATAPULT

Mike's rescue when Mike had bet too much on a pony, then didn't have the cash to cover the debt. And it was tough for James to come up with the cash because he was still a veterinary student. Medicine is a costly commitment, and each time James would bail Mike out of trouble, he knew it was wrong, not only considering his own budget, but he knew he was enabling Mike's addiction.

Finally, upon receiving perhaps the tenth frantic begging-for-mercy phone call from Mike, James hung up and let Mike try to work it out. Mike had actually gone to jail for several months, but the stay – and the inmates – did Mike the favor of letting him see what his life would become if he didn't get help for his addiction.

And when Mike got out, he called his brother first. Rather than being angry, Mike told James how glad he was that James had let him 'rot' in a cell. That afternoon, Mike enrolled in a private inpatient gambling addiction program. He spent several more months behind the walls of the addiction center, but when he got out, he knew he had control of his life again.

Mike realized that he loved the horses, but not just for the love of the race. He wanted to train them, communicate with them, and help others to treat horses responsibly. He apprenticed with the best trainers, and found he had an innate knack with the ponies. After the tragic death of Donald Jenkins, Andrew

CATAPULT

Knightly's former horse trainer, Andrew recruited Mike to become an apprentice trainer at the Knightly Tennessee Walking Horse Ranch and Vineyard. And so, Mike eventually paid off every cent he owed with money earned legitimately from his horse training business.

Mike had been involved with ranchers and vintners in his horse training business, and like a sponge, he absorbed much about ranching and wine growing as he worked with the horses. These days, he spent almost as much time at several local wineries working with the harvest and the bottling as he did with the horses.

But most importantly, what Mike had discovered, aside from love of horses and winemaking, was that had a long-hidden talent for seeing the obvious, something not many people truly possess.

The obvious, in this case, was that not every wine drinker wanted to buy and drink an entire bottle of premium wine, which pours about 3½ glasses. Wines had been bottled in single servings mostly in California, but the wines in those small bottles were somewhat bottom-of-the-line vintages.

Mike thought there was a market for middle- and high-end wines by the single serving, mostly because it would allow a connoisseur to enjoy several of his or her favorite wines rather than limiting the taste buds to 3½ glasses of the same, albeit good, wine.

Although none of the local wineries yet participated in distributing premium "wine-by-the-glass," the concept was taking off in other states and now, if Mike had his way, it would be introduced to the Yamhill Valley.

If the wine growler and boxed fine wine could catch on, and they had done so in a flash, "Vaso de Primo Vino," or "Glass of Premium Wine" could catch on equally.

Mike was on the verge of transforming himself into a significant player in the Yamhill

County wine business, and perhaps the concept was even more far-reaching in its affect. The idea of excellent wines sold by the single serving seemed at the prime time to take off, and after his appearance on a local television show, dozens of investors had contacted him regarding VdP Vino distribution.

Mike had told friends and family that he had accepted as his partner a Japanese former stock broker who, having made his fortune prior to 2000, had then abandoned the market and invested in other securities and land holdings. This mysterious investor had yet to be revealed by Mike, who merely told those who asked that the investor needed anonymity for the time being due to the pending distribution contracts for several local wineries on behalf of a particular company. No one dug too deeply because it was Michael's business, and vintners in the area traditionally welcomed new blood to the fold whether they were hard workers for hire or were interested in making investments in the area.

And the Japanese wine market had only been scratched in the valley.

CATAPULT

CHAPTER 8 -

Every life should have nine cats. *Anonymous*

The local winemakers had a definite interest in the newer Japanese wine market. It was hoped that a group of representatives from Japanese winemakers and distributors would help them connect with this lucrative market.

It's easy to say "wine" in Japanese. It's pronounced the same as in English. That, along with Japan's increased interest in imported wines would make it possible for John Ferguson and other local vintners to sell hundreds, if not thousands, of cases across the Pacific.

Yes, Japan was potentially a lucrative market for Oregon wine. But gaining a foothold was not that easy. Sake, Japan's traditional rice wine, accounted for most of the wine market in Japan. The most popular imports from the past two decades came from France and Italy, which benefited from the global red wine boom in the late 1990s. New World wines from California, Australia and New Zealand had muscled into the market in the past few years.

Locally, Sol Lina Winery had halted wine sales to Japan several years prior due to its takeover by California's Jackson Family Wines. The mass-market winery decided the sales figures weren't satisfying and dropped the Japanese distributor. Sol Lina had also sold bulk Pinot Noir for several years to a producer in the Japanese market, but when the winery didn't have excess wine the next year, that producer found another source. Japan could be demanding and it was hard to sustain the fluctuations in that business.

Earlier in the year, Kats Jory Hills Estate, along with several other Seven Oaks wine producers, received emails from Chan Wine Distributors expressing interest in a renewed market for Japanese distribution of Oregon wines.

At first, they were wary, but they soon learned that Chan was the third largest wine distributor in Japan and its New World wine buyer was interested in these wineries' $30-$35 Estate Pinot Noirs. A deal was offered to sell the Kats Jory Hills label, as well as Red Rim and Glory Days wineries' labels. But those wine producers were not the only ones hoping to expand sales into Japan.

CATAPULT

The Oregon Wine Commission and 22 Oregon wineries, mostly from the Willamette Valley, including Yamhill American Viticultural Areas (AVAs), participated in a multi-day trade and consumer tasting in Tokyo. Kats Jory Hills Estate was among those invited.

Called the Savour Oregon Wine Faire, the biennial promotion was funded through the U.S. Department of Agriculture's Fair Marketing Program. Events in restaurants and retail stores would potentially expose 350 Japanese sommeliers and countless Japanese consumers to more Oregon Pinot Noir, Estate Pinot Gris and Chardonnay.

CATAPULT

William Kent, Kats Jory Hills Estate winemaker noted on the trip that Japan was a sophisticated market. Its consumers liked to hear about specific appellations, winemaking styles and cellar regimens. He opined to his fellow winemakers that Japan was a global crossroads market. A wine featured in a restaurant in Tokyo could help sell that wine anywhere in the world. Information on Oregon's various soils, geography and farming practices was posted on a webpage, japan.oregonwine.org, dedicated to Japanese readers. Japan had been established as one of the top three importers, along with Canada and the United Kingdom. The vast majority of the exported wine was Willamette Valley Pinot Noir.

Still, the perception from many wineries was that exporting to Asia was too complicated, that the demand wasn't there and that the market would not be receptive. But Oregon was finding Japanese wine marketing was not that complicated.

CATAPULT

Then-President Obama's proposal for the Trans-Pacific Partnership was a boon for Willamette Valley wine producers. It would re-negotiate portions of the North American Free Trade Agreement and pave the way for trade between the U.S. and 11 Pacific Rim countries. The agreement would be extraordinarily helpful for Oregon ranchers and farmers as it promised to increase exports to these lucrative markets, including farm products and wine. Unfortunately, newly-elected President Trump would soon begin a quest to quash the agreement.

But Oregon wine producers took the time to work these markets and tell their stories about the soil and sustainable farming and emphasize that Oregon's wine was very compatible with most foods. More Oregon wineries could benefit from exporting, even though it would take further research to know what the market needed and to find the right distributor.

Still, the Asian market held tremendous promise for sales outside of Oregon for all its regions.

CATAPULT

CHAPTER 9 -

If a dog jumps into your lap it is because he is fond of you; but if a cat does the same thing it is because your lap is warmer. *A. N. Whitehead*

Michael Middleton had also left a message on Mary's cell phone, but Mary had heretofore missed the message and the call from Mike due to the events of the evening. She was staying with Kate at the B&B in a special 'spill-over' daybed in the sunroom. The room was kept for those times when a guest showed up with more people than they had reserved space for, or just for nights like these, when a friend or family wished to stay close to Kate.

When Mary finally picked up Mike's message, she began feeling distraught not only because of the murder, but because she was worried about Mike. He'd never just disappeared before, at least not since she'd known him.

The message was odd, not only because Mike rarely called Mary just to chat, but the content seemed to take an evasive path. Mike's message pleaded with Mary to ask James to trust him, asked them not to worry and advised he would be back in town the next day and would explain everything.

Mary decided to call James to see if he had any news about Mike. That she did, and when she heard James' rendition of the message he had received from Mike, she was even more confused.

"I don't understand any of this," sighed Mary. "Why doesn't Mike just clearly state what he's up to? Taking a last-minute trip to California just doesn't cut it – it's a big state. And if something should happen to him, we don't even know who he's with!"

"I agree, Mary, but I don't know what we can do about it now," replied James with an exasperated sigh. "Since Charles was looking for him tonight, I think I'll alert him of the latest on Mike, just so he keeps Mike on his radar. He knows my brother can be a pain at times, but his heart is also usually in the right place. I hope this is one of those times."

"I know that his promotion of the single serving wine containers is of utmost importance to him," said Mary. "I do think he's onto a big venture, maybe bigger than he can handle on his own."

"He's a big boy now," replied James with a wry smile. "I, too, worry about him at times because of some of his history, but he's been quite diligent about keeping his life on the straight and narrow, and I really should have no reason to doubt him now. It's just that something in his recent behavior is a bit off, and I don't want to see him get hurt."

"Well, I for one agree he can handle himself, and I know he has really done his homework looking for investors," said Mary. "I wish there was more I could offer him but this venture is way out of my league."

"I'm sure he'll touch bases tomorrow, and I'll have to give him the bad news about tonight's murder," offered James. "I'm certainly not looking forward to that, but we'll know who the deceased is by then, not to mention who might have committed that heinous crime. Imagine, dressing a dead person up as a scarecrow! It's a good thing it was discovered before the children returned to the Halloween field tomorrow. Thanks to you, Mary – and those wandering cats.

"The catapult has been promised for weeks and I know the local children are looking forward to vaulting pumpkins. But I doubt there will be anyone allowed anywhere near that place until it's been secured and the crime scene folks are done, not that any parents want their children to visit an active murder scene to have Halloween fun. I'm thinking Gerald Hawking will relocate the catapult as he has tons of land on which to do so, maybe even closer to the barn where the haunted house draws so many people."

Mary hung up the phone and immediately called to Kate, who was still cleaning up in the kitchen. Nothing new had come forth from the crime scene, according to Kate, so she advised she was going to try to get some sleep. Mary felt the same way, although she was still keyed-up. Some nice tea might help calm me, she thought, and she began to boil a new pot of water for her nightcap.

James called Charles, who said the same: nothing new to report, but the scene was busy with police, crime scene investigators, the coroner and the medical examiner. Firetrucks, police cars, ambulances, and the ME's van still crowded the pumpkin patch. James felt a bit foolish mentioning Mike's issues at a time like this, but he did tell Charles that he would call him in the morning.

The subject of Mike's sudden disappearance would have to await a time when Charles' full attention could be had.

CATAPULT

CHAPTER 10 -

Cats can be cooperative when something feels good, which, to a cat, is the way everything is supposed to feel as much of the time as possible. *Roger Caras*

George King sat by the late evening fire at his home. He had just received a phone call from the McMinnville Police Department advising him of the gruesome scene next door to John Ferguson's vineyard and Kate's B&B. Of course, as a Yamhill County Commissioner, George was usually one of the first to receive any relevant news in his jurisdiction. George was also the editor of the *Jory Hills Times* newspaper. This was certainly not good news at all.

George started to put his jacket on, and realized the cats were staring at him like he was an axe murderer. "Don't worry, you three. I won't be gone long. I promise you that tomorrow I'll invite several of your friends over for a kitty play date or maybe we can have a cat-together at the shelter."

Mona, Mac and Murphy, adopted subsequent to James Middleton's feral rescue (in consort with Cats Pause Shelter), resided with George King. Rather, George resided with his three feline champions.

Mona Lisa is a tiny tiger cat with big green eyes. Striped like a tiger, Mona's beautiful face would light up a room. A black spot on the tip of her nose is a beauty mark. Mona is the practical cat, always looking for solutions to dilemmas. Mona is mum to Mac and Murphy, who resemble her not at all.

Mona

CATAPULT

Mac, a true Maine Coon, is a long wiry feline with a fabulous length of tail and hair growing out of his feet and ears. He could adopt an owl-like expression and a guttural growl that warns his sister to stop teasing him. He could also undertake a slow, methodical gait, which garnered him the nickname 'Mackie Slow-Walker.'

Mac

Sister Murphy was also part Maine Coon. Unlike Mac, Murphy is petite in stature and solid in composition. She is forever bemoaning her waist size and continuously dieting to try and control her girth. Murphy has the best sense of humor of the three, but sometimes her chicanery irritates Mona.

Murphy

George King was proud to be da' to Mona, Mac and Murphy. With his semi-bald pate and jolly demeanor, George provided a wonderful home for his feline charges.

Now, as George closed the front door, the cats stood at the window and watched him leave.

CATAPULT

We never get to go on any exciting trips with George anymore, moaned Murphy. *I'll bet Mo knows all about what happened tonight, and I can't wait until tomorrow to get the entire scoop from her.*

Me, too! meowed Mac. *I love George but he doesn't understand how morbidly curious cats can be and how we might just choose to misbehave when we can't satisfy that curiosity.*

I think George understands perfectly, replied Mom Mona, always with the mom reasoning. *Perhaps he has our best interests at heart. Imagine, all of us piling in his car in the dead of night and trekking off to a crime scene somewhere. We'll be duly informed by noon tomorrow, and that will just have to satisfy you both tonight.*

The three cats wound their way into the great room and each picked out a furry bed to sleep in. The fire was warm and crackling, and soon the three felines were sound asleep.

CATAPULT

CHAPTER 11 -

Her function is to sit and be admired. Georgina Strickland Gates

At four o'clock the next morning, Kate was in the B&B kitchen preparing breakfast for her six guests. When only five guests appeared at the table at five o'clock sharp, she decided to wait a few more minutes for the missing guest's arrival.

At that very moment, Charles appeared at the kitchen door and beckoned Kate to unlock the latch. Standing as a group on the steps, four men awaited entry. Charles had in tow a local translator whose second language was Japanese, as well as several deputies.

"I'm afraid I have bad news – more bad news as this case may be," offered Charles as he stepped first through the door. "We've identified last night's victim as Sun Yuen Wong, leader of your group of Japanese wine salesmen."

Charles and his group walked through the kitchen into the dining room and advised the Japanese men of this news, while Kate stood stock still in shock.

"I can't believe it!" cried Kate as Charles returned to the kitchen. "The group – all six men – came back here together yesterday afternoon, and we all sat down for a spot of tea before they retired. Sun Wong was alive and well at that time!"

"Exactly what time was that, Kate?" asked Charles.

"It was a little before 4 o'clock, and the group was experiencing major jetlag, in addition to the full schedule touring wineries and wine production facilities all day," replied Kate. "They'd had an early dinner at the Red Door, and enjoyed the cuisine. But they knew they had to rise early today for a meeting and then continue their journey on to South America. How did Sun Wong die, Charles?"

"Well," Charles hesitantly replied, "we think by strangulation as there were red marks around his neck, but the medical examiner will still have to verify cause of death."

The remaining five Japanese wine officials sat in stunned silence at the dining table. Since they all had separate rooms, none was aware that any one of them was missing until this very moment. Suddenly wide awake and disbelieving the news, they all began talking at once, keeping the translator busy as the deputies attempted to take their statements.

"I feel so terrible," sighed Kate. "Sun was such a lovely man, and he has a wife and two children at home in Tokyo. I hope you will be as gentle and compassionate as possible when you notify them, Charles."

"That's already been done, Kate," replied Charles. "And it was George King who made the call. I wasn't aware before early today that George spoke fluent Japanese! His younger sister married a Japanese businessman, and George has visited them several times in Japan. He took it upon himself to enroll in language classes, maybe as a form of sibling rivalry, you know, to keep up with his sister.

"George told me he left the house last night to go to the newspaper, as its editor, to begin coverage of the story. The *Jory Hill Times* only issues three times a week, and the next copy will be out tomorrow. I think frankly that those cats of his drove him out of the house.

"In any case, George was a Godsend this morning. He was at my office at 3am, said he couldn't sleep. Again, maybe the cats, but he arrived just as we got the ID on Mr. Wong and he volunteered to make the call to Mr. Wong's wife, as Tokyo time was appropriate for the call. As a Yamhill County Commissioner, he has diplomatic skills I don't possess, as well as the command of Japanese. I was very grateful for his kind offer."

"Oh, that poor woman," murmured Kate. "I feel so very bad for Sun's wife and family, and I feel a certain responsibility since he was staying with me. Charles, I was being so careful with the cats and I tried to be so quiet so they could sleep – and then Sun was murdered – on my watch! I'm rambling, but I can't help it, Charles."

"Now Kate," answered Charles as he tried to calm his petite friend. "I don't believe there was anything you could have done to change the outcome. We still don't have a motive for this killing, nor do we have any clue as to who might be responsible. Sun Wong must have left the B&B as soon as he got back at 4. We don't know if he left willingly or where he might have gone. That was a pretty sick display though, the scarecrow, I mean. I checked the database to see if there were recorded murders similar to this particular M.O., but I didn't find anything."

Just then the translator returned to the kitchen along with the deputies, while the Japanese men still sat dumbfounded at the dining table.

"I'm going to offer them a light breakfast even though I doubt they'll have much appetite," offered Kate as she began to busy herself out of necessity. "I have some nice fresh fruit, hot cereal, biscuits and tea. Please do let me know if there's anything I can do, Charles."

One of the deputies, Julius, stopped to speak with Charles, and he advised Charles and Kate that he learned through the translators that the Japanese group had decided to cancel their planned visit to South America, and would appreciate if they could stay a few more days at the B&B. This would allow them to be available for questions and to make arrangements to send Mr. Wong's body back to Japan after it was released by the medical examiner.

"Please assure them that I will be happy to accommodate them for as long as a week," said Kate to the deputy. "I do have another small group scheduled to arrive in eight days but at this time of year we usually only host couples, a few at a time. I can certainly move any reservations to another B&B if we're too crowded. I think we'll be fine, though."

"That's wonderful of you, Kate," said Charles as he put on his gloves and hat. "I'll need to be on my way now as we have an active investigation to pursue. There are still several crime scene investigators and detectives in the field next door, so if you could keep the cats... and guests... away from there, it would be appreciated."

Kate gave Charles a wry smile and assured him she would be a good gatekeeper. In addition, she volunteered, Mary had stayed the night and would join her in the kitchen soon to lend a hand.

CATAPULT

Kate didn't notice three little cat faces peeking from under the table. Nor did she see the speedy exit made by Mo, Victoria and Phillip as they tore through the B&B only to sit patiently by the front door. They knew it was only a matter of time before Kate would need to check in at the shelter, and there was no way they were going to be left behind. Mo, especially, felt she must tell her friends of the newest developments so they could begin their own investigation!

CATAPULT

CHAPTER 12 -

When I play with my cat, how do I know that she is not passing time with me rather than I with her? *Montaigne*

True to her daily routine, as soon as Kate had assured her guests they were welcome to stay and had offered them breakfast (it was amazing how even in grief, their appetites had recovered), she made her exit to visit the shelter. Mary was manning the kitchen as she ushered the cats out the front door. Of course, Mo, Phillip and Victoria squeezed in to Kate's Mini-Cooper and took their thrones in the back seat, which was complete with safety crate for them to snuggle in.

John Ferguson stopped by the B&B a bit later and offered to stay with the guests, arrange any transportation they needed, and clean the dining room and kitchen in preparation for afternoon tea. John told Mary that the shelter needed her more than the B&B did at the moment, so he asked her to run along. John was grateful for the fact that the B&B only served breakfast and tea, and the clean-up took no time at all.

Upon arriving at the shelter, Kate had barely opened the car door when the three cats streaked out, made a beeline across the parking lot and pushed their way through the cat door in the front of the shelter.

Georgia, come out! exclaimed Mo as she screeched to a halt in the lobby. *I know you're here because Rebecca's car is in the parking lot!*

Georgia

And I see George King's van out there, too – Mona, Mac, Murphy! Come out!

CATAPULT

Four cats appeared from the bowels of the shelter where they had been visiting with new arrivals, and with a few cats who had been there longer than they should have been. These four felines, along with others like them, bolstered the shelter cats' hopes and dreams, and assured the longer-held cats not to fear, that their forever families were just over the horizon.

It's so good to see all of you but I have so much to tell you! exclaimed Mo. *There's been another murder in Seven Oaks, and this time it was one of our Japanese visitors!*

We heard a bit about that horrible event, said Mona, *as Mary arrived a bit ago, and she and George have talked endlessly about the tragedy. Has anyone been able to locate Mike? He was supposed to meet with the six Japanese men – now five unfortunately – early this morning before their trip, and from what we hear, Mike went off to California last evening without a word.*

No one seems to know what has happened to Mike, said Morgan. *More importantly, the five remaining Japanese men are just at a loss, their families worried and begging them to come home, and a widow is left behind due to this crime!*

We must get started investigating this mess! cried Phillip. *We overheard Charles tell Kate that most likely Sun Wong was strangled. I wonder if the medical examiner has verified that cause of death?*

I don't think they've heard anything from the ME's office yet, said Murphy. *Mac and I have put our whiskers together and have come up with a strategy for this investigation.*

We will need to hitch a ride to the field with one of our humans, said Mac, *preferably the one with the biggest car.*

Just then, Olivia Knightly arrived with her charges, Lady, Señor, Winston and Squeaker.

Squeaker and Winston

CATAPULT

Oooohh, we're so glad to see you! exclaimed Georgia. *We're only missing Diana and Edward, Arbor and Syrah. I'm sure James will bring Arbor and Syrah by here soon and we'll just have to get word to Diana and Edward later as I know the Kensingtons are returning soon from the beach. They took the girls and the cats, too. Those two felines actually like that sea spray and damp air. Brrr.*

Lady and Señor

CATAPULT

Olivia had been watching the interaction with amusement. In her twenties, with long wavy brown hair, big blue eyes and slender build, Olivia was vivacious, cheerful and intelligent, and she could charm any of the animals – or the humans – at her father's ranch.

"Wow, that's a lot of caterwalling you guys," observed Olivia. "I can't believe you could really know what's happened at the Halloween pumpkin field, but if you do, I hope you'll keep your little pink noses out of the way," she scolded half-heartedly.

You think we get in the way! muttered Murphy. *Why, we've helped solve several murders in the Seven Oaks area in the recent past, and there's no reason to believe we don't have the superior faculties to solve this one!*

All eleven cats turned and walked away with their tails held high. What a sight it was as they calmly strolled across the lobby and reconnoitered in one of the larger exam rooms in the back of the shelter.

First, offered Winston, *Olivia was quite upset this morning because Mike has not contacted her as promised, but we did see him yesterday working with the horses at the ranch. It seems he was supposed to meet with the Japanese salesmen early today before they left for South America. He'll have one less person to meet with now that Mr. Wong is dead. Dreadful stuff, the way some humans eliminate an enemy. I certainly hope nothing has happened* to Mike as that would just destroy Olivia. It's not common knowledge, but Olivia is quite smitten with Michael. I don't even think James knows, and he's Mike's brother!

Well then, said Mo. It sounds to me like Mike's venture is not altogether on the up-and-up, or he'd have confided in Olivia, at the very least. He hasn't shared the identity of his sponsor with James or Charles, either. I can understand that Mike might not want the world to know about his plans, but it doesn't seem like this is the kind of thing you keep secret from your loved ones.

I guess we'll soon know, Lady purred. Charles will surely have more information, and the first person he'll confide in is Kate.

CATAPULT

CHAPTER 13 -

Cats are glorious creatures – who must on no accounts be underestimated…Their eyes are fathomless depths of cat-world mysteries. Lesley Ann Ivory

Kate's cell phone rang and she knew immediately by the ring that it was Charles. She and Charles had matching 'rings' and she only called him on his personal cell phone. Likewise, unless there was an emergency and he couldn't otherwise locate her, Charles never called Kate on the shelter cell phone.

"Hello Charles," answered Kate. "I've been hoping to hear from you but I know how busy you are with this investigation. "

"Hello to you, too, Kate," countered Charles as he folded several files on his desk. "Busy doesn't begin to describe it, but I wanted to pass on to you that our initial assessment of Mr. Wong's demise was correct. He was killed somewhere else, strangled as we thought, and his body transported to the field. You know, from the back road on the farm, it's just a short distance from road to catapult, which I suppose was why Mr. Hawking had it installed there in the first place.

"We don't yet understand the significance, if any, of the victim's placement in the field, not only dressed as a scarecrow, but placed at the bow of the catapult. We have established that the clothes Wong was wearing were taken from Mr. Hawking's permanent scarecrow a short distance away in the field. Thank heavens we didn't find anything more gruesome in the catapult shot container."

"What, you mean like a *head*," Kate cried. "I can't believe there is such evil in the world!"

"Well, there is," sighed Charles as he multi-tasked in his office, filing papers and updating computer files. "I have stayed awake nights wondering how a human being gets to the point of killing another human being, or how people commit acts of terrorism killing innocent men, women and children. You'd think I would've seen it all in law enforcement, but not only does it never get less shocking, but people seem to find new ways to torture and maim each other.

"But to the point of my call, according to the remaining five Japanese contingents, Mr. Wong had seemed a bit testy after they arrived yesterday, and they weren't certain why. He'd seemed fine on the plane coming over from Japan. Sun Yuen Wong was reputed to be a very level-headed man, who rarely lost his temper or became out of sorts. They mentioned he spoke with several people on the phone shortly after they arrived, including your father. Do you think he and John had a disagreement?"

"I don't believe any such thing," Kate rather defensively retorted. "You're not suggesting that dad has any connection to this, are you Charles?"

"Absolutely not!" exclaimed Charles as he strapped his shoulder holster securely. "I'm merely pointing out that Mr. Wong mentioned to his group that he had spoken with John, and was concerned with *appearances*, especially since they were staying in your B&B at your father's vineyard. He didn't want other wineries in the area to suspect any favoritism in this visit to wine country."

Kate was still a bit shaken from Charles' first remark, but replied, "In fact, Red Rim and Glory Days wineries have been involved in this venture from the beginning. There has never been any suggestion that one winery could – or would want to – handle the Japanese wine market. So 'favoritism' wouldn't seem to be a factor that would affect the other wineries involved. There may have been wineries that were still vying for a position in the distribution process, however, that I'm unaware of."

"Kate, I should've prefaced my remarks with the disclaimer that I'm in no way implicating your father in this deed – and with the massive market to be served, I can't imagine anyone would truly believe that any one winery, or maybe even any three wineries, could possibly handle the vast commitment of supplying that much wine to the Japanese. So, I agree to your postulation that even the appearance of favoritism should not be a factor in the grand scheme of this distribution project."

"I didn't mean to sound so defensive about my dad," replied Kate, feeling somewhat contrite. "He of course has had experience with trying to supply Japan with enough wine to satiate its appetite, and I know he believes that a consortium would be the most logical way to address that demand. In fact, he discussed with me the other day that Sol Lina has re-emerged in Yamhill County, and they are also willing to combine resources to fill the need."

"I'm glad to hear that Kate," responded Charles, "although I had heard rumors that was the case. And I'll wager your dad and the other vintners in the area have spent many sleepless nights thinking of ways to successfully supply that demand."

"Which is why I don't understand why Mr. Wong would deem merely staying at my B&B as inappropriate or lending the appearance of favoritism," lamented Kate. "And it's too late to ask him now, but I'll assure the other Japanese gentlemen that ALL the wineries in the area are favoring a consortium to supply a variety of wines to Japan."

"I, for one, find it hard to believe that Sun Wong's testiness arose from a concern for appearances," stated Charles. "I'll need to get more in-depth with the Japanese gentlemen to find out about other calls Wong received when they arrived, and whether he had expressed any other qualms about this visit."

"It certainly is a mystery to me, Charles," Kate replied. "But we'll just have to wait and see what exactly the group knows about Sun Wong's contacts yesterday around the time they believed he became upset. I don't know that any of them are thinking clearly at this time, so I'm hoping my father is attempting to calm the waters at the B&B. I'll be heading there shortly and I'll let you know if anything further surfaces related to Sun Wong's recent displeasure."

CATAPULT

CHAPTER 14 -

Most cats, when they are Out want to be In, and vice versa, and often Simultaneously. *Dr. Louis J. Camuti*

Mike Middleton climbed down the stairs from the shiny Lear jet, and walked briskly across the tarmac. It was nearly dawn in the valley, with a light mist hanging in the air. He carried in his briefcase a contract that made him uneasy, and he wanted to run it by James and maybe an attorney before he signed it.

If he signed it.

Clearly, his investor was one hundred percent behind his Vaso de Premium Vino proposal, and he felt utterly elated that at last he would prove to the Seven Oaks community that he could do something right.

Odd, though, that Mr. Wu didn't think it necessary to accompany him back to Seven Oaks today, although it was very generous of him to arrange transportation in the Tomoko Company Lear jet.

The meeting the night before had only included one other person, Hiro Shin, president of Tomoko Company. Mike hadn't known exactly who Chen Wu was pitching his project to before the trip, but it had seemed that Mr. Shin was more interested in drinking wine than taking on the distribution of the VdP Vino project. Of course, since Chen Wu would be the principal investor, Mike was a bit confused as to why he needed to be called to California at the last minute to discuss the distribution process this early in the game. It could have waited a few weeks, or even a few months if his proposed roll-out was accepted. But on the other hand, he supposed that his investor knew best how to line up the suppliers and buyers in any market.

Mike, though, was reticent to relinquish control of his product or to submit to that level of management by an independent contractor like Wu, even if the distribution of the product could be managed by Tomoko.

Mike had begun to have the feeling he was being railroaded.

He knew well that the Japanese market was thirsty for new ways to serve good Oregon wines, and he also knew that Sol Lina had failed previously in its attempt to become sole wine distributor to the Japanese market. Sol Lina had produced premium wine at the time, although since its purchase by Jackson, they had concentrated more on middle-of-the-road varietals.

It looked to Mike more like Wu wanted to negotiate a stranglehold on VdP Vino distribution, and certainly Wu had expressed interest in managing, and perhaps at some point buying Mike's patented concept in the single-serving premium wine business.

Mike didn't like that idea one bit. So, after a fitful sleep and much deliberation on the plane ride home, Mike had decided to slow down and talk to his brother and friends in the wine business about the proposal from Wu – and the inclusion of Tomoko – before he went any further down the road with Wu.

Having finished her volunteer work at Cats Pause, Olivia was just preparing to leave the shelter when her cell phone vibrated.

Her caller ID confirmed it was Mike!

Calming herself inside, she pressed the 'answer' button on the cell.

"Hello Mike," Olivia said before Mike could identify himself. "Are you back in town?"

"Sure am, Miss Olivia," answered Mike. "And I'll bet there are a few people who are ticked off at me for flying out of here so quickly."

"You could say that," said Olivia wryly. "You picked an inopportune time to whisk yourself away, but James, especially, was concerned, more than ticked off."

"Couldn't be helped," gulped Mike as he considered the discussion ahead of him with his brother. "Chen Wu picked me up from home last evening with only a few minutes' warning, and insisted we leave right away to catch a late evening meeting of the 'minds' in California. He intimated that if I missed it, we might miss the opportunity to pitch the single-serving wine project to the Tomoko Company president. He's convinced the company will want in on the ground floor of this project. I didn't see the need for such speed in moving forward, but since Wu is my investor, I didn't see any harm in a free ride to San Francisco."

"San Francisco huh," murmured Olivia, "nice to know where you were – after the fact as it may be. Well it so happens a horrific event occurred last evening right here in Seven Oaks. One of the Japanese wine distributors, it's leader, Sun Wong, was murdered!"

"I don't believe it!" exclaimed Mike nearly dropping his phone. "I hurried back this morning because I was supposed to meet with Wong and the other five Japanese businessmen about incorporation of VdP Vino into Japan Airlines' flight service. They were supposed to leave for Chile today!"

"I understand they'll be staying on another week, Mike," said Olivia, "but I doubt they'll be up to a morning meeting today."

"Poor Mr. Wong," lamented Mike. "I hadn't yet met him, but I'd heard that he was a top-notch businessman, and he was very interested in my proposal, as well. I'm in my car on my way to Kat's B&B ostensibly for that very meeting. I think I'll stop by anyway to extend my sympathies and see if there is anything I can do."

"I imagine that will be appreciated, Mike," Olivia smiled into the phone. "Perhaps you can stop by the ranch later. Your brother will be making a visit to check on a couple of dad's horses later this morning, and I know he really wants to talk to you. Several of us have tried to reach you. Was your phone turned off?"

"Actually, it was but I can see that wasn't the best idea. I missed a week's worth of news in one day. I'm not looking forward to the lecture from my brother," said Mike, "but I will stop by to see you and explain to James what I've been doing. I want to follow up on some training issues with three of the horses anyway."

Olivia hung up on the call, still smiling. At least Mike was safe. But in her mind, she felt his departure was hasty and unnecessarily secretive, and Mike would have to atone for that with James. She hoped the two brothers would discuss their issues rationally. It simply wasn't the time to stir up any worse circumstances.

CATAPULT

CHAPTER 15 -

What greater gift than the love of a cat? Charles Dickens

Mike arrived at Kat's English B&B just as his brother James was also pulling in – driving the Spay Station.

"Hello bro," called Mike to James as both climbed out of their respective vehicles. "I thought I'd see you later at the Knightly Ranch. Sorry my phone was turned off and even sorrier that I missed hearing about Sun Wong's death. I spoke just a few minutes ago with Olivia, and I can't imagine what the others in Wong's group are going through."

"Well, you would've known about all this if you'd left your darned phone turned on Mike," snarled James shooing the indignant Arbor and Syrah back into the van. He didn't want to deal with their issues right now while he had his brother to deal with. "We could've used some help with the remaining five

Japanese men. They will, by the way, be staying on another week to await release of Sun's body for return to Japan."

"I heard that and it's not as though I planned the sudden departure," Mike replied, ready for the inevitable battle with James. It got old, he thought, having to account for his every second to his older brother. Why the heck couldn't he just let him make his own way – and his own mistakes, if that be the case – instead of his constant quest for oversight of his little brother's life. "My investor stopped by last evening and surprised me with the trip as well."

"What time was that," James probed. "You're going to be asked to account for your whereabouts since you didn't check in with anyone else here. Charles is overseeing the investigation, of course, and he'll want to see you right away. What time did you leave town?"

"Mr. Wu picked me up at around 6:30 and we drove directly to the airport," replied Mike. "He had flown up here in the Tomoko company jet earlier yesterday and wanted me to fly back with him to meet with Tomoko's president who was only going to be in San Francisco for the day. I don't know why Wu couldn't have let me know earlier but he didn't, and President Shin wanted to see me before he headed back to Japan."

"Wu, huh," retorted James. "Nice of you to finally share the name of your 'secret' investor. What if something had arisen that required your immediate attention here? As it was, you could've avoided your rush back here to meet with the Japanese as they are all consumed with coping with their losses and with making the arrangements to send Mr. Wong's body back to Japan after it's released."

"I thought I told you my investor's name is Chen Wu. He's a retired Japanese stockbroker who is an independent contractor and investor, and who is also interested in the distribution aspect of my project. This project is an area quite unique to traditional Japanese alcoholic beverage consumption."

"No, Mike, you didn't mention his name," said James, "and you didn't share it with anyone else here either. Makes it look like you're hiding something, or at least like you don't know what you're doing or who you're dealing with."

"Well, bro, I do know what I'm doing," quipped Mike. "I actually know more about viticulture than you do, even though you seem reticent to admit that. You're a top vet, but you don't know everything. Wu is sold on my Vaso de Premium Vino proposal, but I'm still negotiating the brand-name wines that will fill the small containers. For some reason, Wu wants to choose the wines that fill the single-serving glasses, and I've told him I have my own ideas about which wineries will be selected. I'm not at all comfortable with allowing someone else to limit my choices of those wines."

"I'm glad to see that you've done your homework," replied James. "I don't understand, then, why your investor is stubbornly pursuing other avenues when you've already decided what's best for distribution of your wines."

"Neither do I," Mike said. "But I was hoping to learn more from the Japanese salesmen staying here. As associates of Chan Distributors, they can give me direct facts and figures since they have the ear of Chan's president. I liked Mr. Shin of Tomoko, but as I've told Wu, I want to keep the distribution of this product in alignment with the distribution of other wines to Japan from wineries in this area. I need to find out what the real deal is before I sign a contract, which by the way, Jim-boy, I was going to discuss with you. I still want your input, but not if you don't dump the 'little brother is always in trouble' baggage, and deal with me as a professional. I believe I've earned that."

"You're right," sighed James as he let out his breath and took a deep one in return. "I apologize, but in the future, you must reciprocate that trust by actually communicating with me, and with others here who only have your best interests in mind.

"It's starting to get cold out here, and Kate and Mary have returned and are waiting with hot tea inside. Why don't you come in and we'll talk? The Japanese are with Charles at the station right now, and probably will be for the next few hours. Charles wants to talk to you as soon as possible, so I'll give him a call and tell him we'll wait here for him. I've got to get the cats out of the van before they stage an uprising. I think Kate brought Mo, Phillip and Victoria back with her, so that'll keep my felines occupied-at least until they come up with another fish to fry."

CATAPULT

CHAPTER 16

Dogs eat. Cats dine. *Ann Taylor*

James returned to the Spay Station, opened the passenger door and 'released' the two aggravated cats. Better they suffer a bit of indignation, he thought, than I have to go looking for those two sleuths before I could go back to the clinic. They seemed jittery this morning, and all I need is to lose them to the wandering pack visiting at the B&B.

But inside, Mo greeted Arbor and Syrah with purrs and head butts. Phillip and Victoria also greeted the visitors with loud mewling and much tail twittering.

CATAPULT

Arbor

Syrah

I certainly am glad you arrived early, exclaimed Mo. *We've been listening to Kate and Mary and to their updates from Charles. We must find out what Mike was doing yesterday afternoon and whether or not he is at all involved in the gruesome deed of yesterday. I'm still a wreck from that scene last night!*

As am I, meowed Phillip. *I hardly slept a wink all night even though I was protected by all of you and by Kate – and Kate's direct line to Charles Beltz at the station! Why, whoever did this could come back and dispatch all of us just like that!* Phillip tried to snap his clawed toes with no luck, but the other felines knew what he meant.

Phillip

"Goodness, what is this howling back here?" Kate shouted to the five cats. "Maybe it wasn't such a good idea to bring you all here today. You probably still smell tragedy in the air, and are remembering the bustle of activity around here last night."

CATAPULT

All five cats flipped their tails straight into the air and left the room in a straight line, as was their habit, making a bee-line for the cat door at the back of the B&B. They didn't wish to waste time and perhaps be locked inside today.

Still in a line with Mo in the lead, the cats headed for the field next door where the catapult still stood tall and threatening. They were not alone in the field however, as the crime scene investigators were just then wrapping up their evaluations of the scene. They had secured all specimens and photographs and were storing them in their vehicles when the cats appeared from the stand of pines.

"Would you look at that," laughed Jerry, the lead investigator of the team. "Five cats in a row and they seem to be on a mission – and heading straight toward the crime scene.

"Hey, you guys," shouted Jerry, "don't play around here, this is a crime scene!"

As if we're playing, sniffed Victoria. *Our noses can find ten times more clues and evidence than their pitiful eyes can locate!*

CATAPULT

Victoria

The CSIs climbed into their vehicles, still laughing at the sight of the cats marching into the field as though they owned the place. At least it was a moment of levity in an otherwise gruesome and frustrating crime scene processing. They felt they had located little to help the police find a murderer, although they had determined the body had been moved to the catapult from another location. Hopefully when they put together all the evidence they had collected, some clue or clues would emerge.

CATAPULT

The cats watched as the vans and trucks pulled out of the field and headed toward McMinnville where the CSIs would gather and organize their finds.

Look! exclaimed Mo as soon as the cats emerged onto the field. *Over there on the far side of the pumpkin patch, under the hay wagon! I'm seeing empty Vaso de Premium Vino containers on the ground. What in the world would they be doing out here? I don't think Mike has ever visited Farmer Hawking, nor has Mike officially released the product on the market.*

I see them, too, squeaked Syrah. *James said that the release of Mike's product is still weeks or months away. Maybe the B&B guests brought samples over here?*

I doubt that very much, replied Mo, her nose twitching to gain a scent. *To my knowledge, none of the* living *Japanese visitors has been to this field. They aren't much interested in Halloween festivities, and besides, they were touring all day yesterday to other vineyards and wineries and were very tired last evening.*

Well it appears the CSIs were not looking for any evidence around the hay wagon, said Arbor, *but then it is quite some distance from the catapult. Perhaps they didn't think any 'trash' over here could be related to the actual scene itself. Nor would they know that the containers are unique to Mike's project.*

CATAPULT

I for one think we should bring Kate over here and show her what we've found, added Mo. *Although the CSIs might not be aware of the status of the Vaso de Premium Vino's release, Kate sure is. I'm hoping she'll pick up on this clue. What bothers me is that this might also implicate Mike in some way.*

Mo flehming

That's for Charles to decide, meowed Arbor. *Either he will rule out the containers' importance to the crime – or he'll start looking for more clues in that direction. If Mike is innocent of any wrongdoing, he should be able to establish that with Charles. If not – and I too hope he's not involved – Mike may have some explaining to do!*

CATAPULT

CHAPTER 17 -

A dog will flatter you, but you have to flatter the cat.
George Mikes

Mike and James sat down at the dining table in the B&B while Kate, having just arrived, hurried to the kitchen to brew them some fresh tea. She had some leftover scones, also still fresh that she didn't want to throw away, so she hoped they would be hungry enough to eat those, too.

When she returned to the dining room, four human eyes opened wide to welcome the hot tea and aromatic scones.

"Oh, thank you so much, Kate," exclaimed James. "I was so busy feeding my cats and the clinic cats this morning that I forgot to eat."

"I've had tons of coffee but haven't had time to eat, either," replied Mike. "What a welcome sight."

"It's been a rough time," said Kate, "so you need your strength to contribute to this investigation. Besides, I certainly didn't want to waste these last few scones. Please. Eat. I'll be in the kitchen finishing preparation for afternoon tea."

Just then the cats returned exactly as they had left – in single file with tails held straight and high in the air.

The cats sniffed James and Mike and proceeded to the kitchen seeking Kate.

"Well," sighed James, "I guess we know how important we are to those felines. Off to find Kate, no doubt."

Mo turned and sniffed high in the air. *Spot on. We know Kate will understand what we want her to do, unlike you two!*

Kate turned as she heard the meowing coming from behind the kitchen door. Through the cat door came the five cats, all of whom were meowing a terrible racket.

"What in the world? Are you guys hungry or are you just feeling neglected with all this excitement? Methinks you need a little attention."

The cats turned a one-eighty in unison but also turned their heads so they stared into Kates eyes.

"You're giving me the willies! Mo, what is it you want?"

Mo, always the leader of any feline group, started her now-familiar whine, and led the group back through the dining room and out the French doors. And Kate, as usual, followed. As she passed James and Mike, she told them she'd be back in a minute, that the cats wanted to show her something.

James and Mike looked at each other and shrugged. Never question Kate when she's on a cat-related mission.

Kate grabbed her jacket from the hook by the French doors and followed the cats across the lawn, through the pines and into the field. When the cats reached Farmer Hawking's pumpkin patch, they took off at a run and jumped up on the hay wagon. Kate, following at a distance and now breathless, arrived at the wagon a full minute later.

"OK, I got the message that you have something you want me to see," panted Kate as she stood waiting for direction. "What is it Mo-girl?"

Mo jumped to the ground and sat next to the rear wheel of the wagon.

Kate took one look and spotted not one or two, but three VdP Vino containers scattered under the wagon.

"Oh my! Where did these come from? We don't have any in the winery yet, so I know they didn't come from there. Then how did they get here? To my knowledge, Mike is the only one who has these in supply until the official release! I'll need to call Charles immediately, so don't you kitties touch these!"

As if we would...

Kate tapped Charles' number on her speed dial, and he answered on the second ring.

"Hello Kate," he said. "To what do I owe this pleasure?"

"Oh Charles," exclaimed Kate. "If you can believe it, the cats just led me back to Farmer Hawking's field, and I've found three VdP Vino containers."

"What?" queried Charles. "Those definitely shouldn't be there unless Mike took them there. He's the only one in possession of the containers at this point, and he's been guarding them pending the patent he's applied for. Please stay where you are, Kate. I'm three minutes away. And please don't let those cats dig around the containers."

"They're being angels, Charles," said Kate. "And remember, they brought me here. I've already told them to stay clear and not bother the containers."

AS IF WE WOULD...

CATAPULT

CHAPTER 18 -

The trouble with cats is that they've got no tact. *P. G. Wodehouse*

Charles arrived at Hawking's field and pumpkin patch in minutes as promised, and with Kate's assistance, located the three single-serving containers. After photographing the wagon and surrounding area, gloved hands dropped each single-serving container into a separate evidence bag.

"I need to call Mike and inquire as to the whereabouts of all his containers. I'll also need to get a statement from Mike regarding *his* whereabouts yesterday. James mentioned that Mike took off with his investor yesterday without so much as a word to James."

"Mike is sitting in my kitchen," offered Kate, "along with James. Do you want to talk to him now?"

"No," answered Charles. "I will call him later and invite him to my office to discuss the containers. I'll also need to get some information on his investor, as only Mike seems to know anything about the guy. Since you'll be going back to the B&B, I must ask you not to discuss our pending interview. I will explain to Mike when I call him. I only hope he had nothing to do with the containers' presence in the field. You can tell him, though, about the containers. It might give him a chance to take inventory and do his own checking on how they got there."

Charles bid Kate goodbye and left the field. As he climbed into his police sedan he turned and waved to Kate, then began the drive back to McMinnville. His worried expression belied his professional demeanor. A hundred thoughts were going through his head, and he tried to sort them out logically.

How could those containers have gotten into that field? Where was Mike yesterday when Sun Wong was murdered? Mike's investor: who is he and where was *he* when Sun Wong was murdered?

Charles certainly was not looking forward to questioning Mike, and his concern spread over his face like a veil. He'd known Mike forever and hoped – no, he really believed – that Mike had nothing to do with the murder.

CATAPULT

Kate returned to the B&B wearing the same expression Charles had worn when he left the scene. The cats marched along next to Kate, but seemed unconcerned that their formation was lost. Kate was glad for the company.

Why, it was impossible that Mike knew anything about Mr. Wong's murder! He was such a thoughtful, compassionate man, one incapable of such violence.

Mary had arrived at the B&B and had assumed the tea-serving duties. She poured Kate a steaming cup, and graciously offered to finish preparation of the afternoon tea for the visitors. The Japanese men had said they would return to the B&B by mid-afternoon, and were looking forward to hot tea and some restful peace and quiet.

"Well, what was all the mystery about?" asked James. "Did those cats solve another case?"

"Don't be so quick to judge," replied Kate, "because they did discover something interesting over in the field. There were several of your VdP single-serving containers under the farmer's wagon, Mike."

"What? Impossible!" exclaimed Mike. "I've been extremely careful to keep those containers under wraps until I unveil the Vaso de Premium Vino product, complete with premium wines. Was there any wine in the containers, Kate?"

"No," answered Kate, "they appeared to be new, sealed, empty and right out of the carton."

"I think I'll head back to the house," said Mike. "I need to inventory. The only containers removed from those cartons were samples I gave to Chen Wu for the bank's review and for demonstration purposes with Tomoko. And I only gave him a half dozen."

"Well, Mike," said James, "it looks like either the containers found next door were some of those demo's, maybe from your Chen Wu's supply – or maybe someone has helped himself to your warehouse supply. Are you sure you didn't leave any of them laying around or maybe you accidentally left those particular containers at the farm?"

"It may *look* like I left them there," said Mike, "but I assure you, I have been quite careful to protect my idea. I'll let you know what I find out after I inventory at home."

CATAPULT

CHAPTER 19 -

By associating with the cat, one only risks becoming richer.
Colette

James finished his tea and took his cup and saucer to the kitchen where Mary was busy preparing dough for the scones to bake for afternoon tea.

"I will be taking my leave, Mary," said James, "but I will be returning here later to help Kate with her guests. I do have several appointments at the clinic, and I'd like you to be there to assist, if at all possible. If you can leave now, I'll bring you back here afterwards and you can lend Kate a hand, too."

"That would be perfect James," replied Mary. "I'll just finish up here and grab my coat. Kate said she'd like to pop by the shelter with Mo and her other two charges because there were two injured kitties being transported from the shelter today."

"Ahh, those are the same two kittens I'll be seeing shortly," said James. "I examined them briefly yesterday. Their injuries are not catastrophic, but one appears to have a simple fractured of his right front leg on which I placed a temporary splint, and the other some cuts and bumps on his head. It seems they were found playing in the highway. Either someone dumped them or they wandered from a field onto the road."

Mary and James walked down the winding path to the front driveway with Arbor and Syrah in tow, and they all boarded the Spay Station.

Kate, too, finished her B&B chores and loaded three cats into the Mini. Bound for the shelter in somewhat crowded quarters, the cats were amazingly calm.

That is, until Kate pulled into the parking lot of Cats Pause.

As soon as Kate opened the Mini's driver door, all three cats shot out of the back seat on the driver's side and sped through the shelter's front cat door.

Winston! Squeak! squeaked Mo. *I see Olivia's VW Bug outside!*

The three cats entering the building and the two who were already on the inside nearly collided as they rushed to see each other. All five skidded to a stop in front of the reception desk, much to the dismay of several visitors who had come to the shelter to visit, and perhaps adopt a furr-ever feline.

You will find beautiful, loving kitties waiting for you today, meowed Winston to the three ladies sitting across from the desk.

An older gentleman also waited for his 'tour' of the facility. He was seeking a senior cat or bonded senior pair to keep him company, those who would be calm and grateful to find a loving home.

In truth, there were two unrelated cats at Cats Pause who had not transitioned well to shelter life, and even after foster care, were unhappy and withdrawn in the shelter.

In years past, shelters had required a surrender contract when families or good samaritans brought in homeless animals or animals they could no longer keep due to dire circumstances. It was always very difficult for shelter intake personnel when someone would ask if the shelter could let them know if their beloved pet, or the stray they found and carefully transported to the shelter, was not adoptable.

Being unadoptable could take many forms. Sometimes the animal became 'grumpy' and displayed biting or howling tendencies, or they became withdrawn or unsociable or fought with other animals in a group setting. Sometimes they were unable to transition even after being in a foster setting. Failure to transition after trying other options made for an unsafe environment for the animal, the other shelter animals and shelter personnel.

And without a 'call-back' option, shelter personnel had to watch the surrendering person's face fall when they would explain that there were no options for them. Once the surrender contract was signed, there was no more information available to them. A finality, for sure.

No matter what the outcome was for the animal they were turning over, there was a missed opportunity because the shelter could not offer them any peace of mind.

Now, Cats Pause and other well-run animal shelters in Oregon had instituted the "Call-Back Program," a program that allowed the shelter to call the party surrendering the animal and offer the individuals a chance to reclaim that pet if the animal was not transitioning well into shelter life. When surrendering an animal, both owned and stray animals, individuals could now enroll in the program free of charge. Every 'customer' now had the option of signing this additional agreement to become a safety net for the animal they know and love, or for an animal they had found and had become attached to. For a vast majority of cases, this safety net is not needed, but it is nice to know it was there.

But even more importantly, the program empowered shelter employees to address the concerns of community members. The response from the community had been overwhelming positive.

It also gave the surrendered animal a chance to find their forever homes through alternative routes than the humane society – creating a viable positive outcome for animals that previously had very few or no options at all.

In the reception area, Mo and the other four cats walked around each other several times, then turned and bounded to one of the shelter 'visiting rooms' where they could chat in relative privacy. Soon, though, the room would be full of cats and people seeking each other with curlosity and loving intentions.

We have news, meowed Phillip and Victoria in unison.

We, continued Victoria, *led Kate to some important evidence in Farmer Hawking's field that the CSIs either missed or considered unimportant. Kate called Charles and Charles thought it might be important, too, and he was going to call Mike who went home to inventory and swore he didn't leave the evidence in the field! And then James left for the clinic with Mary to take care of two cats who were injured on the highway! Whew, all that in one breath! We have been listening carefully to conversations between James, Kate, Mary, Mike and Charles to try and glean some clues for our own search for this murderer!*

Well, said Squeaker, *Olivia finally heard from Mike, who told her he had been in California with his investor. Mike told Olivia that Chen Wu stopped by with little notice last evening and insisted Mike come with him to California to meet with the president of a distributing company.*

We need to find out when Sun Wong was killed, pondered Mo. *Then maybe we can narrow the list of suspects!*

Well, we think Mike was in the area until around 5:30 last evening added Phillip. *Of course, our humans are all accounted for.*

There are many people we don't have contact with purred Winston, *so we'll have to listen carefully to Kate and the rest so we can piece two-and-two-and-two together. You know we are much better equipped to do that than humans. But getting the humans to listen isn't so easy.*

Just then, Olivia brought six cats, including the two cats who had failed to transition to shelter life, into the visiting room to await their human visitors.

One of the visitors was an older woman who had been feeding a stray cat that she eventually brought to the shelter. That cat happened to be one of the cats that had not been able to transition to shelter life, and shelter staff had called her to see if she'd like to revisit her decision. The shelter also had provisions to assist elder and other adopters with limited incomes, which was the case with this woman. They held open house with barrels filled with cat food at least twice each month. For adopters who did not drive, staff could even deliver free food to their doors. Better to feed the kitties in a loving home than feed and house them in the shelter.

The five sleuths slipped out the door and back to reception area, where they parted company: Mo, Victoria and Phillip to Kate's office where they could eaves drop, and Winston and Squeaker to help Olivia bring the humans to the visiting area.

Mike had just reached his home when his cell phone rang. Charles bid Mike hello and asked him if he would mind coming to the station in McMinnville to help him understand some of the evidence.

"Charles," began Mike, "let me complete my inventory of the VdP Vino containers, and I'll be right there. I gather you're calling about the containers."

"Right," replied Charles. "Go ahead and finish your count. If you're not missing any containers, we'll have to start looking at whoever you might have shared the containers with."

"That's a very short list," said Mike. "I've only given containers to Chen Wu, but I don't know how I'd prove that. Am I a suspect, Charles?"

"Everyone is a suspect until we have timelines and evidence sorted out," replied Charles. "I'll see you here at my office as soon as you can get away. It would be helpful if you can think of any information you have about Wu."

Mike could tell by looking at his container cartons that none of the large boxes had been violated. He counted the containers in the only open carton and found only six missing.

What the...? There were no more missing so he knew the whereabouts of the only ones he had shared; but Mike was more concerned about how he would account for his own whereabouts. He didn't know when exactly Sun Wong had been killed – but his sudden departure for California with Wu certainly made Mike look suspicious.

Well, he sighed, I'll just have to sit with Charles and write down my timeline. I know I didn't do anything wrong, but it sure doesn't look good right now.

So, where the hell is Wu?

CATAPULT

CHAPTER 20 -

Intelligence in the cat is underrated. *Louis Wain*

Charles hung up his call to Mike and immediately called Kate.

"Hello Charles," answered Kate with a smile. "To what do I owe this second phone call today?"

"We've determined Sun Wong's time of death. He died between 4:30 and 5:30 in the afternoon. The body was definitely moved to Gerald Hawking's field, but we don't know yet from where. He was strangled but otherwise not assaulted. He had no bruises except those around his neck, although there appears to be a small wound on his back, perhaps from a stun gun. I'll keep you informed of anything else we find because I know you are concerned for your own safety, as well as that of your guests.

"George King has volunteered to contact your Japanese visitors to give them the most recent information in their language. We don't suspect any of them as their whereabouts are accounted for the entire day."

"Well, at least you've determined Mr. Wong died in the afternoon – and not next door!" cried Kate. "I'll do anything I can to help, Charles, but I'm needed here at the shelter and won't be returning to the B&B to serve our guests afternoon tea until around 4. I know these gentlemen only want peace and quiet, but I feel it is important that I be with George when he informs them of the details."

The cats did not lift their heads, but their ears were perked up and their eyes riveted to Kate and her phone conversation.

"I think you're right, Kate," said Charles. "I'll tell George to meet you at the B&B at around 3:30 so you'll have time to talk with him about your guests. If you think they are too fragile, we'll wait until later in the evening to inform them of our findings. They will have had a rough day."

Kate and the cats motored along Highway 99 to the bed and breakfast. They had enjoyed a late lunch at the shelter, and were thrilled when all six cats who were introduced to the potential adopters left the shelter with their new humans for their furr-ever homes.

CATAPULT

The two 'unadoptable' cats were both taken home by the older woman, Maude, who was the good samaritan who brought one of the strays in. It seemed the two cats, though having no use for any of the other cats in the shelter, had bonded with each other and were stuck together like glue. Both had warmed instantly to Maude and of course, Maude fell in love with both, too. The two cats were ensconced in two small carriers, and shelter staff hauled two large donated bags of dry food and a case of canned food to Maude's car.

I'm glad we had a chance to get to know those great cats, offered Mo. *They will enjoy their new lives because their adopters seemed like enthusiastic people and were definitely cat lovers!*

Agreed, responded Phillip. *I'm very happy for them, and also very happy that we had the chance to update Squeaker and Winston, and then Georgia, who stopped by the shelter. Georgia was going with Rebecca Sherlock and the baby to see George King later, so she will update Mona, Mac and Murphy – if George hasn't already given them the most recent information – inadvertently, of course, hee hee.*

"Goodness!" cried Kate. "I've scarcely had a quiet moment in several days, and now you guys are chattering my ears off, too. What could possibly be so important that it's gotten you so riled? I'll bet you're hungry! I'll prepare a snack for you as soon as we get to the B&B. I'm certain Mary has the tea, sandwiches and biscuits ready for the 4pm serving."

Why does she always blame our conversations on hunger? queried Mo with a chagrinned expression. *There are times I wish I could just whisper in her ear in plain language she can understand. No, we're not hungry!*

Speak for yourself, muttered Victoria. *I haven't eaten since early breakfast and my tummy is growling.*

Agh! cried Phillip. *For such a tiny cat, you eat all the time. I don't know why you aren't big like Mo.*

Hey, snapped Mo at the insult. *I've told you many times, I'm big-boned, not fat, and I can tell you it's simply a matter of metabolism. Mine has slowed beyond belief, but added to my already considerable frame, my muscle tone is superb.*

Mo

CATAPULT

Well, I for one am glad we've reached the B&B and I'll hold Kate to that offer of a snack, quipped Victoria.

"OK guys," said Kate. "Thank heaven we're here. I can't hear myself think! The inside of the Mini is like an echo chamber when you all are caterwauling!"

Inside, they found Mary in the kitchen with finished trays brimming with scones, served with clotted cream and jam and a lovely Battenberg Cake on a cake server, while fruit tarts, fudge brownies and white chocolate truffles graced a tiered caddy. Mary placed cucumber (de riguer!), smoked salmon and egg salad crustless tea sandwiches on a lovely antique English Chippendale platter. Earl Grey, English Breakfast and Paris teas were brewing in three different Royal Albert teapots.

"Well, it's about time," greeted Mary to Kate and the three cats. "Our guests have returned from their rather dreadful day with the coroner and the police. I do believe they are ready to just relax and reflect."

"Oh dear," said Kate. "Perhaps I should call George King and ask him to wait until later to come by to talk with our Japanese visitors. They may need some time to decompress from the gruesome events of the last few days."

"Apparently, George already called them, and they are fine with getting more interviews out of the way," said Mary. "I think they'll be receptive to George being here, but since they're already in the dining room, let's serve tea now."

The two wheeled a serving cart loaded with the trays of warm scones and pastries, cakes, sandwiches and teapots to the cloth-covered dining table. On the second shelf of the cart were serving ware, mixed antique teacups and plates, milk, jam, sugar cubes and cloth napkins.

Meanwhile, the cats stood guard at the back entrance. Should George bring Mona, Mac and Murphy, they wanted to be the first to greet them.

Kate returned to the kitchen while Mary did her best to smile and serve. The Japanese men understood their attempts at simple pleasantries in Japanese, so the serving task went smoothly.

The back door opened abruptly and a blast of cold air, three cats and George King entered the warm kitchen.

We were hoping you'd be able to talk George into bringing you, Mo exclaimed to the arriving Mona, Mac and Murphy.

He made us promise to stay out of the way and not to get underfoot, hissed Mona. *We are* never *underfoot! Rather, these humans are endlessly clumsy and manage to step on our paws and tails and get in our way more often than not. It's not our fault they don't watch where they're going and lose their balance easily!*

Mona

Murphy, who was rather portly herself, immediately squeezed through the cat door to the dining room, followed by the other five.

Murphy

CATAPULT

Mac, the skinniest of the group, slipped through the door with ease, although his long tail was nearly caught when Kate started to open the door. She caught herself and laughed at the mass exodus.

Mac

Three cats are a lot of cats in a room; six cats can be overwhelming.

George and Kate joined the group in the dining room, and, having given the cats very stern looks, watched as they all sat primly in a far corner where they posed as though they wouldn't be a bother.

"*Konbanwa* (good evening)," George greeted the five men in Japanese, all of whom bowed in greeting. "As I advised you earlier by phone, I'm here to give you an update on several aspects of Sun Wong's murder that you may need to relay to his family, and certainly to his business contacts and the Japanese police.

"First, Mr. Wong died between 4:30 and 5:30 in the afternoon. Since we've established your whereabouts for that time, as well as the hours before and after, please be assured you are in no way suspected of committing this crime.

"Second, Mr. Wong was strangled, but there do not appear to be any signs of a struggle or defensive marks on his person. This does suggest that he knew his attacker, although the attack must have been sudden and unexpected. He may have been disabled by a stun gun.

"And finally, I do need to ask you all whether Mr. Wong mentioned anything unusual, anything he was concerned about, or if you noticed anyone suspicious hanging around when you arrived here. These details may seem insignificant, but could be extremely helpful to the police in their investigation."

The Japanese men looked at each other, shrugged their shoulders and displayed their palms. They advised George they had been asked similar questions at the police station, and they had answered all those questions completely – *wakarikiru*.

George explained that he was aware of their interviews, but perhaps they'd had time to reflect, and since they were back at the B&B,

they would not be feeling pressured or rushed to amend their statements.

The men looked at each other: one man, Quan, volunteered that he had thought it was odd that Chen Wu, a former stockbroker and a current independent contractor working with Tomoko Distributors, had contacted Sun Wong as soon as they'd arrived. They all knew Chen Wu from prior business dealings, and they knew he was not part of this project.

"Then Mr. Wong spoke with at least one other person besides John Ferguson? Can you give me a description of Chen Wu, and perhaps do you know his whereabouts?" George asked.

"No," replied Quan for the group. "It has been many years, and we only know that Sun was NOT friendly with this man and he had a very short, terse phone conversation with Mr. Wu immediately after we arrived. But one other thing. Sun had called Wu by a rather derisive name: *Kakashi – Scarecrow.*"

CATAPULT

CHAPTER 21 -

Cats are rather delicate creatures and they are subject to a lot of ailments, but I never heard of one who suffered from insomnia. *Joseph Wood Crutch*

It was true that Mike had been seeking premium wines to fill his VdP Vino glasses, but he also sought out the unique wine, often made so by selective processing.

He was, in fact, attracted to a certain few wineries, other than Kats Jory Hills Estate Winery, Red Rim and Glory Days, and those few boutique wineries produced unique premium wines utilizing unconventional methods.

One such winery was his favorite, its small batch production unable to fulfill the number of orders that Mike envisioned, but making it a perfect member to add to his unique 'Vaso Club' of several select varietals.

Chinook, a winery in Yamhill-Carlton, Oregon offered a down-to-earth Pinot Noir as a specialty. This Pinot Noir was produced using only technology that was available in the 19th century.

At harvest, horses hauled the fruit to the winery, where the grapes were de-stemmed and pressed manually. Hands and feet are employed to punch down the fermenting cap of grape skins.

A bike-pedal-powered pump transferred wine from wooden fermenter to wooden barrel.

Barry Dunne, Chinook's wine-making proprietor, packs four cases of Project 1898 Pinot Noir into waterproof bags in early September, loads them onto a horse-drawn wagon and drives the wagon over gravel roads toward the town of McMinnville. There, bicycle messenger Jaime Martinez loads the wine onto his cargo bike and pedals it to the banks of the Willamette River. Dunne and cellar assistant Joseph Anson secure the wine in a canoe the next morning and paddle it down the Willamette River for three days, finishing their journey in Portland.

"We made it, 73 miles altogether," Dunne reported. "Five miles by horse, probably three miles by bike and the rest by canoe."

For Dunne, the journey by hoof, pedal and paddle was a statement about what kind of winery Chinook is. "We are really serious about making wine in a historical fashion," he said.

Despite its $65-per-bottle price, Project 1898 sells out quickly each vintage. Because in a sea of Pinot Noir, it's something different, if not exactly new.

"Next year," Dunne said, "we're going to put buckskin seats in the canoe."

Another boutique winery that aroused Mike's interest was Calliope, a small single-vineyard winery located just outside Dundee.

Calliope also crushed grapes each year by hosting an Oktoberfest Grape Stomp in September. The grapes are de-stemmed prior to the event, with numerous stomping applicants vying for prizes by producing the most liquid.

The final crushing and straining processes are completed by a single cellar assistant, who then funnels the wine manually from the fermenter into barrels of all types. The winery produces barely 50 cases of fine Pinot Noir. Again, as a Pinot Noir, it was a not-so-unique wine in the Yamhill Valley, but the processing employed a unique (and joyful!) winemaking tradition. These wines also sell for around $60 a bottle, but the fine taste makes the purchase more than worthwhile to local oenophiles.

Mike had never any intention of locking in one winery for his project, no matter how premium the wines, to realize his VdP Vino dream.

Chen Wu, however, had seemingly been unaware of that intention – until Mike made clear on this last trip that the smaller boutique wineries in conjunction with several larger wineries would be his preference to fill the VdP Vino glasses.

Chen practically accused Mike of abandoning his friends, namely Kate and John Ferguson as well as their winemaker, William Kent, to deal directly with several small, unknown wineries. Mike knew that John did not expect – nor did he want – a monopoly on the VdP Vino wine introduction. John's winery, Kats Jory Hills Estate, was blooming with more wine sales than it could handle, now to include mass distribution in Japan, even while many newly planted vines were maturing. Those vines would not be ready for a first bottling for five years. In addition, John had agreed to supply several cases of his own Estate Pinot Noir for consumption in the VdP Vino venture, so he had not been excluded at all. Rather, John had bigger fish to fry.

Chen's desire for lack of variety confused Mike. He was, however, annoyed and concerned that Chen might back out of his investment promise or lose interest in the venture before it ever got going.

Now, though, Mike sat at his small desk in his small home office with a worried expression. What good would be his ideas if he wound up in jail – for something he certainly didn't do? He just had to convince Charles that he didn't kill Sun Wong. He had no alibi for the time of the murder as he had been alone at the Knightly Ranch working with the horses. And he and Chen Wu didn't leave the ground for California until around 7 that evening.

What will I do if no one believes me?

CATAPULT

CHAPTER 22 -

Prowling his own quiet backyard or asleep by the fire, he is still only a whisker away from the wilds. *Jean Burden*

James looked at Mary as they finished mending the two injured kittens. He and Mary had agreed the cats needed quiet time to heal, so he planned on keeping them at his clinic for a week or so to assess their progress. The cats had seemed quite sociable, and as soon as they were on the mend, he would take them to Cats Pause for intake to foster care as a pair, where they could mend further and be quietly assessed for adoption. He had already placed their photos on social media as "found" cats, as he had determined they were not micro-chipped.

He bedded the cats in two small cages so they would be unable to thrash around or worry their wounds – or each other – when they awoke. They looked so peaceful, and he had every confidence they would be as good as new.

James turned to Mary and sighed in relief. "I'm so happy these two are going to be alright, and even happier that Mike has returned, that he seems to have his head on straight, and he's working with Charles to figure out Sun Wong's murder."

"I absolutely know he had nothing to do with Sun's murder," Mary replied, "but I'm afraid he'll have to establish his timelines with the police before they dismiss him as a suspect."

"Well, I'll do all I can for him," James said as he disposed of his gloves and operating gown. "I'm sure Wu's pilot filed a flight plan at the McMinnville Airport, so we can check to see what time the plane left. I'm quite sure it left *after* the time of the murder, so the trip would not rule out that Mike – or Mr. Wu, for that matter – had been in the area when the 'opportunity' occurred."

"I'm sure Mike is aware of that too," replied Mary, "so he'll have to establish his whereabouts during the precise time. I hope he had actual contact with someone. He's been so secretive that even Olivia, who has been privately seeing Mike for a few months, says he doesn't confide in her."

"He's been dating Olivia? Why am I the last to know these things? But that's a great idea, Mary," posed James bravely, although feeling a bit left out. "Maybe Olivia has some idea where he was – or was supposed to be – and we can 'walk back the cat' from there."

"Odd you should use that expression," replied Mary. "I was thinking almost the same thing. He can establish with someone, anyone, where he was at a certain time, like the flight departure, and then work backwards from there. Much the same way Charles and Company investigate a crime."

"It's getting late, Mary, and I know you're getting tired. Can I talk you into dinner tonight?" asked James. "I'd like to take a break from this madness and enjoy a nice steak with a bottle of Seven Oak's finest Pinot Noir."

"I'd be delighted. First, though, you'll need to run me back to Kats B&B to pick up my car. Perhaps you can pick me up at my house around 6:30?"

"It's a date," said a smiling James who was very much looking forward to the evening.

In fact, he had something else very special in mind.

After James dropped Mary at the B&B to pick up her car, Mary decided to run inside to say hello to Kate.

George and the cats were still there, and Kate and George sat at the kitchen table discussing the meeting with the Japanese.

"Mary!" exclaimed Kate. "Please come in. We think we have a clue in Sun Wong's murder."

"I can only stay a second," replied Mary. "James and I are having dinner at 6:30, and just look at me. I'm a mess!"

"First of all, you're never a mess, but we have reason to believe that Chen Wu may somehow be involved in Sun Wong's case," confided Kate. "Apparently, Sun knew Mr. Wu from previous business dealings in Japan. The other Japanese here weren't exactly sure why the two didn't get along, but Wu called Sun when the group first arrived here. They told us that Sun disliked Mr. Wu – and that he called him by a derogatory name, "Scarecrow!"

"And if that isn't enough," said George as he rose from the table, "the two had an argument the same day Sun was murdered. I do wonder if Wu has an alibi for that time? Well, enough conjecture. I've got to stop by McMinnville PD on my way home to apprise Charles of this news. I'll just collect Mona, Mac and Murphy and be on my way."

"I'll follow you outside," said Mary. "But I'll see you first thing in the morning, Kate, to help with breakfast. I do so enjoy your Japanese visitors but I certainly miss Sun Wong. He was such a lovely man."

Sitting quietly in a corner of the kitchen, the cats just stared as if there was a bug on the wall. The humans could not possibly be aware of the tension among the six felines.

This was huge news.

The Scarecrow may have constructed the Scarecrow!

And what does a Scarecrow do? It guards its territory. Perhaps this Scarecrow was guarding his own secrets!

CATAPULT

CHAPTER 23 -

Cats know how to obtain food without labor, shelter
without confinement and love without penalties. *W. L.
George*

Mary put the finishing touches on her
makeup – not that she wore very much makeup
on her face – and settled down in the living
room to await James' arrival.

A moment later, James pulled into
Mary's driveway, not in the Spay Station, but in
his older model Lexus. The car was ten years old
but looked like new, except for the obvious lack
of design changes of the new models.

James jumped out and bounded up the
steps to the front door. Mary pulled the door
open so quickly James nearly fell into her. Both
laughed at the obvious: they were excited to
see each other.

"I'm taking you to our favorite
restaurant," confided James as he righted

himself and regained his balance in Mary's foyer. "Tina's, in Dundee. I have reservations at 6:45. I know we don't go there as much as we'd like because it's rather expensive, but heck, I love spoiling you!"

Mary laughed and hugged James in greeting. "And I love being spoiled, especially by you, James. Do you like my new sweater? I got a fantastic deal online. It's cashmere and oh so soft. I just loved the color, too: periwinkle."

"It's gorgeous, as are you," cooed James. "It brings out the color of your eyes and makes those eyes sparkle. I'll be the envy of every other guy in Tina's tonight. Let me help you with your coat. You were smart to wear a sweater as it's rather chilly this evening."

James ushered Mary to his waiting car and off they drove to Tina's, a small but very desirable dining establishment that specialized in French and American cuisine.

Arriving on time, James dropped Mary at the door while he parked the car.

The restaurant was warm and inviting, and they were seated immediately at the best table in the house. A tuxedo-attired waiter/sommelier brought lemon water and a bottle of Kats Jory Hills 2011 Estate Pinot Noir, their favorite.

The waiter uncorked the bottle and poured a taste for Mary, who swirled the delicious aromatic wine slowly in her glass, and

---

inhaled the scents of wild berries, oak and chocolate, before sipping.

"Lovely!" Mary praised the wine to the sommelier, Luis.

"Before we toast, I'd like to present another surprise," said James. "I do so hope you like it."

The waiter brought a small plate of truffles. One of the truffles, a chocolate mint crème, sat atop a small box.

James presented the box and truffle to Mary, who lifted the truffle off and opened the box without hesitation. Inside was the most beautiful diamond engagement ring Mary had ever seen.

"Oh James," Mary gasped. "It's so beautiful! I just adore it. Will you slip it on my finger?"

"I will if you will say you'll marry me, Mary," replied James. "Huh, marry me Mary. I do like the sound of that."

"As do I," Mary gushed, "and yes, Mary will be delighted to marry you, James!"

"Whew," James exhaled as he placed the ring gently on Mary's finger. "I was hoping you would accept my proposal. I know you well enough to know that you'd never reject me, in public, at least, but there's that horror males harbor of taking the walk of shame as his lady storms off in pure rejection."

"Yes, you do know me better than that," blushed Mary. "I can't believe men still carry those old junior high insecurities, but I do understand the fear of the unknown. You also know I love you to pieces and can't wait to be your bride."

The waiter brought two glasses of Tina's finest champagne for the lovebirds' engagement toast. Each wrapped an arm around the other's arm and drank from the other's flute.

"To my fiancée," toasted James.

"To my fiancé," Mary returned.

"Well, now we have the pleasure of telling our friends," said James. "Shall we invite several friends to my – in the future to be our – house tomorrow?"

"I don't think I can wait to tell Kate, probably tonight!" cried Mary. "But with this murder hanging over our heads it feels like a weird or inappropriate time to celebrate, even though I'm happier than I've ever been and want to share it. You can tell Mike and Charles tonight if you like. I'd rather wait and host an engagement soirée in a few weeks, if you agree."

"Mary," replied James, "anything you want to do is fine with me. It's settled then. Will you please wear your ring before the formal announcement?"

"You couldn't pry it off my finger with a wrench and a crowbar," laughed Mary.

"Good enough," sighed James in relief. "Boy, I was starved when I arrived here, but my nerves have gotten the best of me. I think I'll just have the crab salad tonight."

"Not me," said Mary as she picked up the menu. "All the excitement has made me very hungry. I will order the filet mignon with a loaded baked potato."

Both James and Mary sailed through the remainder of the evening with smiles on their lips and tenderness in their eyes.

At the end of a perfect evening, James took Mary home and although he hated to say good night, he knew she wanted to savour the evening's events privately.

And he couldn't wait to call Mike and Charles to tell them the good news!

CATAPULT

CHAPTER 24 -

If a cat did not put a firm paw down now and then, how could his human remain possessed? Winifred Carriere

The following morning, Seven Oaks was buzzing with the news of Mary's and James' engagement. Delighted friends called and stopped by the clinic to offer their congratulations.

Mary and James, however, carried out the usual chores of the day. Mary arrived at Kats B&B to help with the breakfast presentation, but she was wearing her new ring and couldn't help looking at her left hand often. A euphoric James drove directly to the clinic to check on his two surgical charges.

Mary had called Kate the night before as soon as her feet crossed her front door threshold. Kate was ecstatic and promised to begin planning an engagement party for her dear friends.

CATAPULT

James had called both Charles and Mike, and the usually reserved veterinarian bubbled over with happiness at Mary's acceptance of his proposal.

Mike felt a sort of relief at the news, not only because he wanted his brother to be happy, but that some good news at last had arrived. Although he had congratulated both James and Mary, Mike's mind was still busy figuring out how he could establish an alibi for the time of Sun Wong's murder.

On the afternoon of the murder, he had stopped by the Knightly Ranch to check on a few of 'his' horses, but had seen nary a human soul during his stay. He hadn't given it any thought at the time because he became engrossed in tending and training the horses. James was proud to train these horses, and in direct opposition to treatment of Tennessee Walkers in the southeastern United States, allowed the horses to frolic in the fields and wear standard hoof attire.

Mike and Andrew Knightly agreed wholeheartedly that 'soring' was a cruel, barbaric procedure applied to Tennessee Walking Horses.

Soring, as the term implies, is a practice in some states that involves the intentional infliction of pain to a horse's legs or feet to force the horse to perform an artificial, exaggerated gait. Caustic chemicals – blistering agents like mustard oil, diesel fuel and kerosene – are applied to the horse's limbs, causing extreme pain and suffering.

A particularly egregious form of soring known as pressure shoeing, involves cutting a horse's hoof almost to the quick and tightly nailing on a shoe, or standing a horse for hours with the sensitive part of his soles on a block or other raised object. This causes excruciating pressure and pain whenever the horse puts weight on the hoof.

The life of a sored horse is filled with fear and pain. While being sored, a horse can be left in his stall for days at a time, his legs covered in caustic chemicals and plastic wrap to "cook" the chemicals deep into his flesh. In training barns where soring takes place, it is common to see these magnificent horses lying down in their stalls moaning in pain.

Soring has become a very common and widespread practice in the Tennessee Walking Horse show industry for decades. Although illegal, the practice has been allowed to continue, especially in Tennessee, Kentucky and other states in the southeast where judges *reward* the "Big Lick" artificial gait, thus encouraging participants to sore their horses and allowing the cruel practice to persist.

The Horse Protection Act of the 1970's banned the cruel practice, but underfunding and political pressure from industry insiders have plagued the USDA's enforcement of the practice. As a result, states were allowed to train and license their own inspectors to examine horses at shows for signs of soring. Apart from a few who are committed to ending soring, most of these designated qualifying persons, or DQPs, are made up of industry insiders who have a clear stake in preserving the status quo. To add insult to injury, as soon as Donald Trump became president, he signed a bill allowing the soring practice – and other deplorable practices – to continue unabated.

Both Andrew and Mike shuddered at the cruelty of this practice, and lobbied hard in the Oregon Legislature for more oversight in Performance and Racking shows in Oregon. The Knightly Tennessee Walkers were unfettered and happy horses, requiring simply more attention to training to learn the high-stepping gait. Mike was able to work with the horses on a regular basis, and his hard work was rewarded with Knightly Tennessee Walkers winning numerous awards at Performance shows nationwide.

Now though, Mike wondered if he could establish his good deeds and free himself from suspicion in Sun Wong's murder.

If only the horses – or, unaware of the possibility by Mike, the Knightly cats – could talk.

CATAPULT

CHAPTER 25 -

A cat sees us as the dogs...A cat sees himself as the human.
Unknown

One of the first things Mary did – and checked off her list – was to call Olivia.

Mary had been thinking about her volunteering efforts for a very long time. She never had enough time to give to the animals, and she tried to cram too many things into a day: helping at the B&B, volunteering at Cats Pause, volunteering at the Community Pet Food Center, and working at James' clinic, The Cats Meow.

Now that she was engaged, Mary thought it a good time to move forward with her volunteer efforts. She had always thought that working with a spouse, or in this case, a fiancé, was not the best idea for either party. She wanted to be able to share her own experiences with James at the end of the day. If she stayed at the clinic, they would continue to share mutual experiences, but the closeness of that work with James might dampen the joy of seeing each other and sharing unique times at the end of the day – and if she stayed, she still wouldn't have enough time for herself and her volunteer activities.

She had already spoken with James many months ago about her passion for volunteering, and she had also introduced to him her desire to find someone else to help at the clinic in her place.

Olivia was talented, compassionate and excellent with animals, and she had expressed on more than one occasion that she would love to continue her studies in veterinary medicine and find employment in that field.

Although Olivia was excellent with the horses, Mike spent much time with the horses (by choice) and Olivia was relegated to more banal duties. Although she wouldn't want to give up those chores (mucking stalls, feeding and brushing the horses), she had confided in Mary that it was time to move forward, too. But she would need a job before she could save enough to return to school, and even then, she thought she'd limit her studies to nights and weekends.

In her call to Olivia, Mary put the offer over the top when she told Olivia that not only would she be gaining experience in the animal healthcare field, she could bring her cats to work whenever she pleased.

That did the trick for Olivia.

Mary would talk to James again, and she would set up an appointment for Olivia to speak with him about that employment. Of course, Mary would stay on at the clinic until everything was caught up and Olivia felt comfortable taking over her duties as bookkeeper, veterinary technician, and appointment scheduler at the clinic.

At the Knightly Ranch, Olivia was reeling from the invitation to assume Mary's duties at The Cats Meow. And she could take her wonderful cats to work every day if she chose! As usual, Olivia talked to her cats as though they could reciprocate the conversation.

"Oh, you guys," Olivia gushed. "I'm so thrilled that I may be able to work in a field I love and get paid for it! I'll still do my share here at the ranch, and you will still keep your mouser duties. But you'll also get to be ambassadors at the clinic – like Mo is at the shelter – to help frightened and injured cats to be more comfortable in their stays. And you'll get to see Arbor and Syrah daily."

Winston, Squeaker, Lady and Señor rubbed their heads on Olivia's feet and ankles, nearly tripping her in their quest to give her cat love.

I'm so thrilled for our Olivia, meowed Lady. *She loves these horses, but I've noticed lately she's been in sort of a funk with little to do. Mike so adeptly handles the horse training, and when he's here, he takes on the whole package, including the feeding and cleaning.*

Lady

Yes, agreed Señor, *Olivia has not had enough to do, and she's the type of lady who needs fulltime work and fulfillment in her day.*

Señor

CATAPULT

"I hope I'm not boring you," Olivia said to the cats. "You go out of your way to talk to each other, but I hope you're listening to me as well. The big news for you is that you, too, will have quality duties to keep you busy. I'd hate to leave you here day after day when I'm at the clinic as I'd miss you so much. You will be an absolute boon to the clinic's intake of kitties. Remember how frightened you are just going in there to get your shots?"

Yes, I do remember, thank you, said Winston. *I was traumatized for several days, and all James did was check me over and administer my shots. Actually, Mary gave me the shots but I don't hold that against her.*

And do you recall when you had that upper respiratory infection, Lady? Squeaker asked. *Why you were practically catatonic with fear going to the vet.*

Winston and Squeaker

CATAPULT

It's a natural reaction, defended Lady. *Any animal is afraid of going to the vet. First, there's that ride in the carrier. And we all know that tone of voice the humans get when they know we won't like something. They try to soothe and it ends up scaring us to death.*

Then there's the smell of the clinic itself, enough to paralyze an animal for days. Finally, there's the indignity of taking our temperature and other exams that I simply abhor. Not to mention if an animal is sick or injured, they just know they're going to have to endure other procedures and indignities.

"So, I can assume due to your chatter that you agree to the schedule and are up to the challenge of the ambassadorial tasks?" asked Olivia as she laughed at herself. Honestly, talking to the cats, she thought. How could they possibly know what they're in for?

"Now the other thing I must do today is to try and help Mike," Olivia shared. "He appears to be a suspect in Sun Wong's murder because he took off to California without a word AND because he can't establish his whereabouts on the afternoon of that crime. I didn't see him that afternoon so I can't vouch for his whereabouts."

Oh, but we can! screeched the cats in unison. *Mike was here with the horses. We saw him! He was here for hours!*

"Something obviously struck a chord with you all," mused Olivia. "That kind of racket can only mean you're all riled up about something. What in the world is it now?"

We must find a way to show Olivia that Mike was here all the time, cried Winston, *so he couldn't have murdered Mr. Wong!*

It's a shame Olivia doesn't have Kate's intuition with cats, moaned Squeaker. *She and Mo have a sort of telepathy where they connect even if they're not in the same room.*

We must find a way to guide Olivia to proof that Mike was here, whatever that may be, said Señor. *Let's put our heads together and see what we can come up with.*

At that, all four cats turned tail and headed for the barns.

"You guys are just too odd," Olivia called after them. "I guess I'll have to do some sleuthing on my own."

So, on that day, cats and a human set off in their own ways to prove Mike was innocent.

CATAPULT

CHAPTER 26 -

The cat has too much spirit to have no heart. *Ernest Menaui*

Chen Wu sat in the plush lounge of Tomoko Distributors' San Francisco office.

How the hell did Wong surface in the U.S. and not only rise from the ashes but at the most inopportune time? Wu ruminated over the events of the past few days and began to formulate a resolution to yet another problem: Mike Middleton.

Some twenty years prior, Chen Wu was a master stock trader in Japan.

After gaining top status and his clients' trust, he secretly began siphoning millions of yen from the fund using illegal insider deals. One of his top clients, Sun Wong, became a victim of Wu's fraud and embezzlement schemes. When Wong discovered the truth, he immediately filed a lawsuit, but they settled before the case reached any courtroom. During his own investigation of Wu, Wong discovered that Wu's nickname in the market was "Scarecrow," because Wu managed to make deals just minutes before the other traders, thus leading them to believe Wu had some inordinate skills that scared off potential catastrophic failures of nearly impossible trades.

Sun Wong had not been completely satisfied with the outcome of the settlement, although his accounts were made whole and he was compensated fairly for the matter.

Sun Wong was very concerned that Wu had other victims.

Wong followed Wu's business dealings and discovered that even after being caught in the act, Wu was still cheating his customers. Just as Wong had gathered sufficient evidence to take to the commissioners, enough to put Wu away for a long while, Wu disappeared.

Sun Wong searched for Wu for several years, but finally moved on and became one of Japan's top negotiators in mergers and business deals. He later accepted a contract to lead the sales and distribution department of Chan Wine Distributors as Vice President of Sales and Marketing.

Wong was involved in the first attempt to import wines from the Willamette/Yamhill Valley area but became disenchanted when his own company overruled or ignored some of his recommendations regarding distribution. Sun

CATAPULT

Wong knew that no one winery could possibly supply adequate wine for Chan's purposes, but Chan went ahead and contracted with Sol Lina for sole distributorship of its wines. Sol Lina, of course, was unable to supply adequate amounts of wine for the Japanese market, and tried to sub-contract a good portion of its orders from other wineries, including Kats Jory Hills Estate Winery. It still could not supply the requested amounts and qualities of wine, and the Japanese public lost interest. None of this set well with Chan, and the project was mutually dropped.

Now, here again was an opportunity to gain a stronghold in Japanese wine distribution, but starting at a much less ambitious level. Wu had learned that the market could absorb as much wine as the U.S. could supply, but he had a much different approach for this round.

Wu had discovered Mike Middleton's Vaso de Premium Vino project merely by accident. Middleton had been seeking investors for the project through social media when Wu saw the plea and immediately contacted Mike. Wu offered Mike the total investment cash support requested, in exchange for anonymity until the deal could be finalized. Mike Middleton was overwhelmed by the offer, although he thought at the time it too good to be true. But it would be so much easier having one investor to placate, rather than several – or several hundred – had he made his plea through Crowd Rise or some other mass funding venue.

Then, after such careful planning of his entry into the Japanese wine market, Wu got wind of the Chan Distributors Japanese sales expedition to Oregon, and up popped an old nemesis' name as head of the contingency, Sun Wong! As soon as the Japanese group landed in Portland, Wu phoned Wong and tried to divert the Japanese group from the Willamette/Yamhill area. After all, they could do the same type of business in the Southern Oregon Valley or even in Washington by importing different wines, but the scarecrow wanted them to away from his "territory."

Wu and Wong exchanged words. Sun Wong threatened to expose Chen Wu's past to anyone who would listen. Wu tried to keep calm, and assured Wong that his current business dealings were all above-board, that he'd left his past behind, had become a better man. Wong considered this, and against his better judgment, agreed to meet with Wu immediately to clear the air.

Unfortunately, Wong did not share the meeting event or location with the other five Japanese salesmen, and went off on his own to meet with Chen Wu.

As Wong entered the warehouse meeting site, Wu stunned him from behind and strangled Wong with a piece of rope. Wu had briefly visited Kats Jory Hills Estate Vineyards area that day while looking for Wong, and had witnessed Gerald Hawking's introduction of the giant catapult into his field. Wu stuffed all 136 pounds of Sun Wong into a large, solid plastic bag, secured the ties, put him in the trunk of his rental car and drove him to Hawking's field. After taking the bag from the trunk, Wu placed Wong in front of the catapult, removed Wong from the bag, and stuffed the plastic bag into his computer case.

Wu even pondered placing Wong *in* the catapult bucket, but decided instead to dress Wong in the field's resident scarecrow's clothes, to add a touch of the macabre. Besides, it was like projecting his namesake onto Wong. None of the foolish Americans in this area knew his history or that his former trading nickname referred to this guardian of the fields.

And after getting rid of this threat, and with only one more stone in his shoe, the road would be clear to catapult to the top of the Japanese boutique single-serving wine market.

Chen Wu, the ultimate narcissist, loved parody and satire.

And when the deed was done, Wu quickly deposited three of Mike's loaned VdP Vino containers under the hay wagon in Farmer Hawking's field. So much for that stone in his shoe.

After making a first furtive phone call, Chen Wu phoned Mike Middleton and notified him – as he approached Mike's house – that an important meeting in California required his attendance, and he whisked Mike to the airport and to California in the Tomoko company plane. He knew that Mike's sudden departure would place suspicion, on him along with discovery of the planted single-serving containers. And Wu's first phone call had assured a local farmworker a large payment to verify his presence some twenty miles from the crime scenes at the very time of the crime.

CATAPULT

CHAPTER 27 -

We have a theory that cats are planning to take over the world, just try to look them straight in the eye...yup, they're up to something! <u>Dog Fancy</u>

Mike didn't know exactly where to begin. As he sat in the McMinnville Police Station lobby waiting for Charles to return from a deposition, he went over in his mind his activities on the day Sun Wong was murdered.

He'd seen many of his friends in the morning that day because he'd decided to visit a few wineries in the area to further cultivate his VdP Vino idea. He'd completed his site visits at about noon, and then stopped at the Knightly Ranch. He'd hoped to see Olivia as well as the horses, but since she was nowhere to be found, he had to make do with the company of the horses and cats that afternoon.

He quickly adapted to his disappointment because the horses simply enchanted him. He took four Tennessee Walking Horses out to a small pasture and began working with them without ropes or bridles. The horses responded so well to his benign form of discipline, that the human became one with his equine partners. So engrossed in this endeavor was Mike that he lost track of time. He finally took the horses back to their stalls, brushed and fed them, and made some notes about his progress on the wall charts he kept. He was exhausted but content, as were the horses, so he gladly bid them good day and drove to his home for supper.

That was it. Ranch, home, supper without seeing another human soul until Chen Wu stopped by to pick him up.

Charles parked his cruiser in the police lot and came through the back door of the station. A sergeant saw him enter and told him that Mike was waiting in the lobby, so Charles headed that direction to find Mike.

"Charles," said Mike as he spotted Charles striding down the hall. "I'm here to give you the statement you requested. Is there somewhere you'd like to go to talk?"

"Hello, Mike," Charles responded as he extended his right hand in greeting. "Yes, let's go to my office."

CATAPULT

The two left the lobby and entered Charles' office, where Charles closed the door.

"Have a seat, Mike," offered Charles as he rounded his desk to his own chair. "I don't think this will take long, but we're questioning everyone connected in any way to Sun Wong in this case. You know that we found three of your VdP Vino containers at the crime scene, correct?"

"Yes, so you've all said," replied Mike. "But Charles, I didn't leave them there and I've kept a very close watch on those containers until I have my patent in place. I take some with me on sales calls and those are all accounted for."

"Have you loaned or given any of the containers to anyone else?" asked Charles as he made notes.

"The only person I've trusted with my containers is Chen Wu," replied Mike, "and that's only because he is my investor in the project. He told me he needed a few as proof to provide to the bank to establish he was investing in a new business."

"Hmm," mused Charles. "You do realize that you previously neglected to share your investor's name with anyone, including your brother. James may be a bit overbearing, but I suspect it's only because he still feels responsible for you, even though the rest of the world sees you as an entrepreneur and businessman now."

"I think that's my mistake, Charles," confessed Mike. "I felt I had a lot to prove given my prior incarceration and addictions. I guess James should've been the one I trusted."

"It's a common result of family dynamics," replied Charles in a more conciliatory voice. "I'm sure James understands, and if he doesn't, it's incumbent upon you to have 'the talk' with him."

"Agreed," sighed Mike. "And next on my agenda."

"But you're certain no one, not even James, has access to those containers?" Charles asked. "They're fairly small and perhaps you placed a few around when you made sales calls at the wineries."

"Nope, I can account for all but the half dozen I gave to Wu," said Mike.

"You won't mind if I accompany you to take some photos of your inventory as well as any invoices for their purchase? I need to document those for the record," stated Charles.

"You're more than welcome to do that, Charles," said James as he fidgeted in his chair. "Have you checked the containers you removed from the field for fingerprints? Mine are probably on them, but if they were stolen there may be other prints as well."

"The containers are at the lab and the print results are due back later this afternoon," said Charles. "We could see some smudged prints on them when they were found because of the dampness in the field, but the techs will do their work to see just whose prints those were."

"I just don't know what else to do, Charles," said Mike with a palpable tension in his voice. "I had nothing to do with this, I think you know, but I don't have a single person to vouch for my whereabouts from noon to 6pm on the afternoon of Sun Wong's murder."

"Of course, I believe you had nothing to do with Sun's murder, Mike, but we have to consider everyone and everything that came near Sun Wong when he arrived here. We're also testing other objects from the field for prints," Charles said as he closed his notebook. "We found prints, lots of them, on the catapult and its bucket and even some latent prints on the belt from the scarecrow. All this will be evaluated and reported by the crime lab."

Mike sighed and started to rise from his chair. "I hadn't the chance to meet with Sun Wong yet, Charles, but I don't have any way to prove that I didn't see him alone or at all that day. Please let me know if you find any other prints on the VdP Vino containers, Charles. I know you won't find any of mine on anything else in that field as I haven't visited Gerald Hawking or his seasonal display yet this year."

"I will keep you apprised, Mike," said Charles. "I know how deeply affected you are by all of this, not to mention being traumatized by what you may construe as aspersions being cast upon you in the community. You'll have to admit that your sudden departure on the day of the murder, as well as the discovery of those containers in the field does point an accusatory finger at you. We need to establish your innocence by a process of elimination."

"I know," sighed Mike. "Walking back the cat..."

Mike left the station and headed to the only place he could think of that made him feel safe. Knightly Ranch and the horses and Olivia. He needed to clear his head and put some perspective into this mess.

CATAPULT

CHAPTER 28 -

It is remarkable, in cats, that the outer life they reveal to their masters is one of perpetual boredom. *Robley Wilson, Jr.*

Winston, Squeaker, Lady and Señor had spent their time indulging in their favorite pastime: barn moussing. After a fairly productive afternoon, the four felines sat on a bale of hay in the sun, grooming and licking their paws. Squeaker also had the benefit of a good grooming by Winston. The two were usually inseparable, although Winston would at times become petulant when Squeaker displayed her independence by taking off without him, especially when he was being lazy and she wanted to play with Lady and Señor.

That sun is so welcome this time of year, mewed Squeaker as she used her damp paw over and over to clean her face and head.

No doubt it's what drew all those mice out of their mouse holes, drawled Winston trying to stifle a yawn. *That was a delicious repartee and I'm wont to take a nap over in that sunny corner.*

Not just yet you don't, remonstrated Lady. *We have the advantage of our noses and our senses to really encompass and overturn the whole of this ranch for clues to help Mike. Olivia told Kate that Mike swears he was here at the ranch when Sun Yuen Wong was murdered — and we saw him. We need to supply his alibi!*

Lady

I do whole-heartedly agree with you Miss Lades, meowed Señor as he, too, groomed and licked his feline fur. *Let's throw ourselves into this investigation before Olivia comes home. We need to find something we can show her to help Mike — and time is of the essence.*

CATAPULT

Señor

The cats began their search. They decided to start in those places Mike frequented when he came to work with the horses. They combed each stall. The horses were amused by the four little felines, and greeted them in each stall they entered. In turn, the cats showed their trust and friendship for the horses by weaving in and out of their legs and letting each proud equine know that they had swept the barn clean of mice, something the horses appreciated. They hated to find mouse droppings in their food, and the mice would build nests in their straw. Most repugnant to these stately Tennessee Walkers.

CATAPULT

I think we've combed the horse stalls as much as possible, said Squeaker.

You're right, replied Winston. *Now, though, we need to refocus. Mike always kept a table and gear in the tack room. Let's go check that area out next.*

The cats made their way through the barn to the tack room. The room was loaded with saddles, blankets, brushes, shovels and various other horse tack, some of which was hanging on the walls where bridles and chaps could be found, or sitting on wooden 'horses' where the saddles rested. All the tack was well organized, as Mike and his predecessor, the late Donald Jenkins, needed to quickly find items when saddling horses for training. The easiest way to quickly find those needed pieces was to always return the items to the same place they were found in the first place.

CATAPULT

Mike's chair was adorned with two jackets and a flannel shirt. On the floor in a box were several pairs of boots, extra clean socks and boot cleaners.

Mike had recently brought a small card table into the tack room. On it he kept records of grain, hay and tack purchases, as well as training records.

On the wall above the table was a calendar of sorts, on which events and times for training were recorded. Because Mike was paid an hourly rate, he was required to keep track of his time spent with the horses, as well as what was accomplished at each timed event.

The cats immediately honed-in on the calendar.

Look! exclaimed Lady and Squeaker simultaneously. *There's Mike's timesheet and training record on the wall. And look specifically at the day Sun Wong was murdered...Mike recorded that he was here from 12:30-5:30pm and he's documented exactly what he did with the horses on that day!*

That's proof Mike didn't kill Mr. Wong, hissed Winston. *The man couldn't have been in two places at once. Of course, Andrew or Olivia will need to verify that the entry was made on that date during that time, and that it wasn't added or tampered with if Mike was here after that time.*

The four cats' tails quivered in the air with excitement at the finding of Mike's training documentation. They grouped into a pack and ran from the tack room, bounding across the barn floor and the barnyard, directly to the house. They instinctively formed a line at the cat door at the back door to the ranch house, with Winston leading the way.

Inside the house, the howling began as they searched for Olivia. As luck would have it, Olivia had just returned from the shelter where she had been speaking with Mary about working at the clinic. The cats spotted her just as she was about to admonish them for the howling.

"What in the world?" scolded Olivia. "You scared me to death with your screeching! I should just separate you into two rooms and let you consider your behavior more quietly!"

The four cats were suddenly silent, and looked as though they were smiling.

Well I never, sniffed Winston. *You'd think we just howl for the fun of it!*

Sometimes we do! laughed Winston.

We got her attention anyway, chided Lady. *Let's circle her legs and feet and then dart back out the door. Olivia's sure to follow!*

Olivia, was indeed startled by the cats' howling behavior. She had been preoccupied thinking about Mike and also about her day volunteering at the shelter. She was worried about Mike but ever so elated over the six adoptions that afternoon.

CATAPULT

As she started to deal with the cats and their noise, they suddenly circled her feet and shot out the back cat-door.

Of course, Olivia followed.

The cats made a beeline to the barn with Olivia on their paws. They didn't slow down until they reached the tack room. Then all four cats jumped onto Mike's makeshift desk and began meowing.

Winston leaped onto his hind legs and scratched at the wall next to the calendar. Lady followed suit, and put her paws directly on the calendar.

"Well, I'll be," said Olivia. "What are you two pointing at if not the calendar? I've never seen such a dramatic display of 'look where our paws are' than this!"

Olivia stepped closer to the calendar and the proverbial light bulb went on.

"Oh yes!" she cried. "Mike's calendar! He documented that he was here on the day of – and during the time of – Sun Wong's murder! I remember now that father commented to me about Mike's schedule with the horses that evening! He specifically told me he would write Mike's paycheck the next day since he'd put in so many hours – and on the day of the murder. Look, there's dad's initials next to the dates and times Mike worked! "

That's all we needed to know, meowed Winston. *If both Andrew and Olivia can vouch for Mike's documentation on that day and at* that time, then Mike couldn't possibly have murdered Sun Wong. He was here all the time!

It's too bad the horses can't tell the humans, hissed Squeaker. That would have saved a lot of time and trouble. Ah, but horses don't have our wiles.

"It looks like you guys have saved Mike's bacon," Olivia commented to the four cats. "I didn't put two-and-two together until just now. Thank you all! I'll call Mike – and Charles, and let them know what you've so adeptly pointed out."

The cats calmed down and sat together preening. It could be said they had satisfied, yet smug expressions on their faces.

But really, Olivia thought, how could they possibly know?

CATAPULT

CHAPTER 29 -

When you are looking, a cat acts like a princess, but the minute they think you are not looking, a cat acts like a fool.
KC Buffington

Charles was just wrapping up a query on a burglary when his office phone buzzed.

Chen Wu was in the waiting lobby asking to speak to Charles.

"Well, give me a minute," Charles told the sergeant in charge. "I'll come retrieve him shortly."

Charles tidied up his desk, closed files and locked drawers. The he walked the short distance to the lobby area where Chen Wu was sitting.

When Charles appeared, Chen Wu stood and extended his hand. Charles accepted the handshake and asked Wu how could he assist him on that day.

CATAPULT

"Lt. Beltz, I've just returned from California and heard the dreadful news about Sun Wong! I've come to see if there's anything I can offer to help you find his killer."

Charles cleared his throat, and asked Wu if he'd mind accompanying him to his private office. Chen Wu accepted the invitation.

Charles closed his office door and Wu seated himself across the desk from Charles' chair.

"Thank you for coming in," Charles said to Wu as he pulled his chair closer to his desk. "Just how do you think you can help this investigation, Mr. Wu?"

"Well, for one thing," offered Wu, "I understand you are interviewing people who knew Wong to establish alibis. I'd like to offer mine for the record."

"That would be a big help," replied Charles taking out his notebook and digital recorder. "Where were you on that date between two and six in the afternoon?"

"I was in Newberg at Sol Lina's vineyard working with one if its employees, José García, and we were discussing a potential contract which would include Sol Lina's wines in the Japanese trade agreement. We had coffee and I toured the facilities with José for several hours between four and just before six o'clock. You're welcome to call Mr. García to verify my account."

"It's very kind of you to volunteer your statement, Mr. Wu," said Charles. "That saves me time in this investigation. Then you won't mind if I follow up on your statement with Mr. García?"

"Of course not," exclaimed Wu. "That's the reason I stopped by today. I'll only be here for a day or so and I have many calls to make. I thought it would be more expedient if I volunteered my statement rather than waiting for you to call me if you wanted to arrange a meeting."

"Is there anything else you'd like to state for the record?" Charles asked Wu. "I've taken notes, and of course you see that your conversation is being recorded. That way your own words are in the record without me putting my own spin on them, however inadvertently."

"No, that's all I had to say, Lieutenant," replied Wu. "Yes, I'm aware that our conversation is being recorded and thank you for your time."

At that, Wu rose from his chair and again extended his hand. He advised Charles he could find his own way out, and off he walked down the hall and out the front door without looking back.

Interesting, mused Charles. I wonder how Wu knew I'd be interested at all in his statement of his whereabouts? Odd he didn't volunteer any history with Sun Wong. I wonder if he knows he's a suspect, along with anyone else who can't establish his – or her – whereabouts that afternoon?

Charles picked up the phone and dialed the number Wu had provided for José García.

After Chen Wu left the McMinnville Police Station, he sat in his car and made a cellphone call.

Mike Middleton answered on the first ring.

"What do you want, Wu," Mike growled into his phone. "You conveniently appear and disappear when it suits you, but I suspect you've planned those moves well. I have a lot of questions to ask you."

"Now Mike," soothed Wu as he started his car to warm the interior. "I've only just landed so I stopped by the McMinnville PD. I'd like to speak to you about our friend, Mr. Shin. I confess that he's not expressed interest in your project, and I'm sorry I wasted your time hauling you to California to speak with him."

"That's no surprise, Wu," groused Mike. "It was clear to me during our one conversation that he has no idea what my project is about. He's after a different kind of investment."

"Well, that's sort of what I wanted to discuss with you, Mike," Wu responded. "I haven't had much luck convincing wine dealers that your project will take off. So, to protect my investment, I'd like you to sign that contract assigning me control of the product's distribution. To that end, I don't want a whole bunch of wineries to keep track of. I want one winery assigned to fill the VdP glasses, but filling the glasses with a variety of that winery's top wines."

"That's not acceptable, Wu," said Mike as he felt the heat generating under his collar. "That's never been and never will be the deal. I don't want to contract with just one winery, and I want – and made it clear I've always wanted – unique, high-end wines from several wineries to fill my containers."

"Mike, you're so naive," snarled Wu with a derogatory guffaw. "You'd just let those wineries dictate prices. With one winery filling the glasses I can control prices."

"Well, Wu," answered Mike barely controlling his anger, "we don't have a deal, you and me. I need you to return the sample VdP containers I loaned you. I'll just keep looking for an investor or investors who acknowledge and support that it's my idea and I'm the boss."

"I'm sorry to hear that, Mike," said Wu. "Perhaps we can still talk about this, and I'm happy return your containers. How about meeting me at the old mill warehouse? I'm storing some personal wines there. I have some business in that area, and it's close to you."

"I'll see you in an hour, Wu," said Mike as he calmed down a bit. "And don't forget to bring those containers."

CATAPULT

Mike felt a foreboding sense of something he couldn't quite put his finger on, but he wanted his containers back – more to see if any were missing from the small supply he'd loaned Wu than just wanting them back for his inventory. Mike shook off the feeling, and decided to call Charles to let him know about the meeting and the return of the containers. He knew Charles would be interested to know, too, if any containers were missing.

Wu hung up the phone and put his now warmed car into gear.

That stupid idiot, he thought about Mike. If he thinks I'm going to tip my hand about the containers, he's mistaken. Besides, I don't fully trust García to back up my alibi. Methinks I was correct: Mike Middleton has outlived his usefulness.

CATAPULT

CHAPTER 30-

There is the little matter of disposal of droppings in which the cat is far ahead of its rivals. The dog is somehow thrilled by what he or any of his friends have produced, hates to leave it, adores smelling it, and sometimes eats it…The cat covers it up if he can. *Paul Gallico*

Chen Wu's seat in Charles' office was still warm when Charles started making calls, the first to José García, who volunteered to come to the department to see Charles.

He then called the Japanese wine salesmen who were still staying at Kat's English B&B because he wanted to follow up on George's report about Wu's association with Sun Wong.

The group, via its spokesman, Quan, voiced its unanimous opinion that Sun Wong was not fond of Chen Wu, but they had no information on any past the two might have had. Except that Sun called Wu 'Scarecrow' just before his death.

Charles then performed a computer search on Sun Wong's history, hoping to uncover something, anything, of significance.

And there it was. Sun Wong had sued Chen Wu in Japan some years ago, and the case had been settled. Charles was able to access closed records due to his status in law enforcement, and he soon discovered that Wong and Wu had a previous business relationship having something to do with the stock market.

Mike had said his investor, now known to the community as Chen Wu, was a former stock trader/investor. From the legal documents, Charles could piece together the complaint: Wong accused Wu of fraud and embezzlement.

To Charles, that meant that Wu's stock dealings allegedly were not on the up-and-up, and that he also either siphoned monies from Wong via the stock exchange or he blatantly took dividends and/or interest that did not belong to him.

The fact that they settled probably meant that Sun Wong did not want to engage in protracted litigation. Perhaps then, the amount of money was not significant, not that it mattered except as a link to potential punishment.

But Sun Wong had seemed to be such an honorable man. Why hadn't he pursued Wu so that he wouldn't be able to repeat the offense with other investors?

Hoping to find the answer to that question, Charles dug into Chen Wu's history, as well.

From that research, it appeared that Wu had simply disappeared from the stock market – and Japan – barely a year after the lawsuit was settled. Perhaps Sun Wong simply couldn't locate him after that, or he didn't have the resources at the time to track him down.

In any case, Charles thought it was no wonder Wu had earned the 'Scarecrow' title.

And perhaps Wu was so arrogant of his own abilities that he didn't think anyone would perceive an analogy between that nickname and a scarecrow left at a murder scene? Was the scarecrow in the pumpkin patch a symbol, that it guarded Wu's secrets much like it guarded the field? Or was Wu simply a supercilious sadist hoping to lead police on a merry chase, thinking he could outrun and outfox the law?

And was there a connection to the catapult? It was clear that the scene at Hawking's field was staged. Did Wu think that he, as the Scarecrow, could rid the world of Sun Wong and that it would somehow catapult Wu to some new level? Doing what? The mystery continued.

CATAPULT

Oliva couldn't wait to tell Charles about the calendar and the newly discovered proof that Mike was at Knightly Ranch when Sun Wong was killed.

Instead of picking up the phone, though, she decided to make the short trip to the McMinnville PD to talk to Charles, and she would take the calendar to show him, as well. The fact that her father had witnessed and dated the notation the evening Sun died was proof that Mike hadn't added it later or that it had been tampered with in any way.

She'd tried to call Mike, but he hadn't been available, and she didn't want to leave such an important message in voice mail. She had also noted on the calendar that Mike had been to the ranch that very day before the cats led her to the calendar. She was sorry to have missed him. And she did miss him!

When she arrived at the police station, Olivia grabbed the calendar and went to the lobby. She waved at several people she knew outside, and the desk sergeant ushered her to Charles' office immediately. Everyone in McMinnville was acquainted with Olivia to some extent, some because of her father's ranch, others because of her involvement with her father's wine sales, and still others because of her commitment to Cats Pause Feline Shelter. Olivia would go door-to-door during fundraisers for the cats, and she always left behind a little gift, even if the recipient chose not to make a charitable donation.

"What a nice surprise, Olivia," welcomed Charles. "On a day when I've had contact with several less-than-desirables, it's a joy to have you seated in that chair."

"Why, thank you, Charles," laughed Olivia. "I've brought you something else I think you'll enjoy even more than my mere visit."

Olivia handed Charles the calendar and then explained why she brought it to him.

"I was doing some chores at the ranch, and the cats started acting very strangely. You know those four, Charles, always into something and moussing their lives way. Anyway, the cats nearly tripped me trying to get me to follow them."

While Charles listened to Olivia, he mused how similar to Kate was Olivia, especially with respect to cats – and to her belief that cats had some kind of special knowledge of human goings-on. What will it be this time, he wondered, as he smiled at Olivia.

"Charles, I see that look," admonished Olivia. "You may pooh-pooh the cats' innate penchant for sensing the bizarre, but I do believe they think, know and sense things on a level we can't possibly understand.

"In this case, those cats led me directly to the tack room. And I don't mean they just pointed their noses that way, they almost pushed me across the barn, the four of them tangling themselves around my feet and legs. Then the rascals jumped up on Mike's small desk and put their paws on that calendar. I swear it's true, Charles!"

As Olivia spoke to him, Charles was looking at the calendar. There on October 3 was Mike's training schedule for that date, documented from 12:30-5:30pm and initialed and dated by Andrew Knightly.

It appeared Mike had an alibi for Wong's murder.

"But Olivia," Charles thought out loud, "Mike could have added this or changed it after Sun Wong's murder."

"Not a chance," replied Olivia. "Father commented to me on the evening of October 3rd that Mike had been there that afternoon, and he knew that because he stopped by the barns looking for Mike. He went to the tack room and saw the calendar where Mike had written his schedule. That entry had not been there at noon when dad was in the barns, and dad was looking for Mike around 6pm. I guess he just missed him – both times."

"Do you mind if I keep the calendar?" Charles asked Olivia. "I'd like to add this to other evidence we're gathering in this case. This is especially good for Mike, because he said he didn't see a soul at the ranch that day and felt that no one could back up his visit. Well, not a soul except those cats, obviously."

"You see?" Olivia smiled at Charles' slight wavering of his opinion that it wasn't scientifically possible for cats to know what was happening in the human world, except when it came to dinnertime. "I didn't think to look at it, and even Mike seems to have forgotten about it. Those cats just knew it would help Mike if we had the calendar in-hand."

"Well, I owe those cats a special treat the next time I'm at the ranch," laughed Charles.

"I spoil them so badly anyway, Charles," offered Oliva feeling slightly embarrassed. "I confess that I was so happy about their calendar revelation that I gave all four of them some tuna before I left."

"Well, I'll think of something special," said Charles as he rose to walk Olivia to the door. "Thank you so much for stopping by, Olivia, and yes, do give those cats a big cat-hug for me."

CATAPULT

CHAPTER 31 -

One of the most striking differences between a cat and a lie is that a cat only has nine lives. *Mark Twain*

After Olivia left the department, Charles' next call was to a rental car company. He found, not surprisingly, that the car Chen Wu had rented on his October 3rd trip to Seven Oaks had been cleaned and rented again. The car was, though, in the rental lot now, so Charles sent a deputy to impound the car and begin finite testing.

José García was prompt in his meeting at the department, and Charles offered him coffee in his private office.

The farmworker appeared intimidated by Charles, but more likely, he was intimidated by being in a police station after being summoned. The man's hands shook as he drank his coffee, and although he'd been in America for close to twenty years, his command of the English language was still less than perfect.

The first question Charles asked of Mr. García was, "Where were you between two and six o'clock on October 3rd?"

José couldn't look Charles in the eye. Again, though, not unusual for a farmworker to be shy and intimidated by law enforcement, especially since many migrant farmworkers were singled out in immigration investigations around the area.

"Señor Beltz," began José, "I was working in the vineyards and winery of Sol Lina on that day. I worked from five in the morning until six that night."

"Did you see Chen Wu on that day," asked Charles.

"Sí Señor, he came to the vineyard to see the boss," said José again looking at the ground.

"I know he came to the vineyard," replied Charles, "but others I spoke with out there said Wu made a morning visit and never did see the owner. Did you see him in the afternoon?"

José fidgeted in his chair and began coughing. Charles offered him some water, but he declined. When he got control of his cough, José straightened in his chair.

"Señor," he said with a sad and frightened look on his face, "I did see him that morning, but even though Señor Wu asked me to say I saw him in the afternoon, I did not. Please do not be angry with me. The man makes me afraid and he said that if I did not say he was at the vineyard in the afternoon, he would call INS and tell them my wife and daughter are illegal! I swear they are not, Señor, but just having to defend ourselves with immigration officials is so very stressful for us! My daughter was born here and my wife and I have been in America for many years. We do not want to go back to Mexico!"

"I believe you on all counts, Mr. García," said Charles, "but since Chen Wu has signed a statement swearing he was at Sol Lina that afternoon, I will need you to sign a statement contesting his statement, and attesting to your lack of knowledge of his whereabouts that afternoon since you did not observe him at Sol Lina."

"I will gladly do so, Señor Beltz," José stated, "but please do not let him come near my wife and daughter. They are defenseless. My wife works in the fields with me and my daughter is completing the fifth grade. They are in this country legally and if you like, I can prove it to you."

"Did you not provide that proof to your employer when you came here?" Charles asked the man. "And if your daughter was born here, does she not have legal status?"

"Of course," replied José, "but it is so embarrassing and threatening for them to be questioned constantly about their status. They have done nothing wrong and I wish to protect them."

"Be assured they will not be bothered, José," said Charles as he stood to shake García's hand.

José also stood and thanked Charles for his kindness. Charles led him to the sergeant's desk where he was instructed to make himself comfortable while his statement was being recorded. Charles told him that after he signed his statement, he was free to leave and to rest assured his family would not be harassed in any way.

After José García's departure, Charles returned to his office and continued reading the background history on Chen Wu he'd pulled earlier.

Chen had been in the United States for about 20 years, arriving a year or so after the scandal in Japan that was spearheaded by Sun Wong. After he'd arrived in America, Wu had promptly applied for citizenship, which was granted several years later. Apparently, background investigations in that era were less stringent than they were today, as nothing had been uncovered about Wu's shady dealings in Japan.

Wu had become a resident of California, but had also become quite adept in 'brokering' contracts between growers of various crops and distributors of those crops. He specialized in contracting grapes from California vineyards to local wineries, and garnered a reputation for sealing lucrative contracts for distribution of the wines.

About five years ago, Wu had branched out and had taken an interest in Oregon wines. He started his sales and distribution contracting in Southern Oregon where the warm-climate heavier wines were produced.

Later, he moved operations north to the Yamhill and Willamette valleys where he developed a taste for local Pinot Noirs. He did not maintain an office in the area, preferring to use the more fluid California facilities owned by the distributors he worked with.

But Charles noted that Wu did maintain his own private wine cellar at a warehouse in Newberg. It was featured in a three-year-old spread in *Wine Country,* which also included reviews of another 12 collections in the area.

As he organized his search priorities, Charles called the lab to request expedited processing of Wu's rental car and the VdP containers.

The investigation had picked up speed, and Charles was certain he would soon have Sun Wong's killer in custody.

But Charles could not help but reflect how odd it was that Mo and her feline friends led their humans to the VdP Vino containers in

CATAPULT

Gerald Hawking's field, and the Knightly cats were credited with leading Olivia to Mike's calendar. There just might be something to that fabled sixth sense in cats, Charles thought.

CATAPULT

CHAPTER 32 -

If you yell at a cat, you're the one who is making a fool of yourself. Unknown

While waiting for the lab to report back, Charles got to thinking that Chen Wu's warehouse wine cellar might be a good place to visit. He wasn't even sure why he wanted to see it, but he couldn't sit still and wait for the lab while he could be considering new areas that might provide clues in this case. Finding the warehouse connection online was new and could be important, and certainly Wu had not volunteered the location or the fact that he occupied space there.

The crime scene investigators had pretty much combed through the pumpkin patch and its bizarre collection of Halloween sights. Charles would release the field back to Gerald Hawking the next day so that the farmer could resume hosting kids and families in the

---

spirit of the season. Hawking would move the catapult to another area, away from the crime scene's taped-off area, although Charles had given him permission to remove the tape because they were finished with the investigation there. The newspapers had been not at all graphic with respect to the staging of the scarecrow at the catapult and Sun Wong's murder investigation scene, thanks to George King.

So, to the families and children around the area, they would simply be visiting Farmer Hawking's wonderful Annual Halloween Haunted House and Corn Maze. And they would enjoy catapulting pumpkins for prizes with no concept of the bizarre event that had occurred there on October 3rd.

Of course, though looking into the warehouse was a good idea, if Charles wanted to thoroughly search Wu's wine cellar, he would need to obtain a search warrant. But he wouldn't need a warrant if he just stopped by to see if Wu was there, and maybe asked Wu to show him around.

And that's exactly what Charles would do after he finished completing his reports. Well, maybe after he downed his boxed lunch, thanks to Kate. He'd been looking forward to those scones all morning.

CATAPULT

CHAPTER 33 -

Charles had just finished his custom-catered lunch when the lab returned his call.

Lab tests showed rope strands, traces of plastic and unidentified hair traces in Chen Wu's rental car trunk. Of course, those could have been left there by anyone who rented the car. In addition, there were two sets of fingerprints on the VdP Vino containers, Mikes and an unknown print. There were also several sets of unidentified prints on the scarecrow's belt.

There were no traces of Sun Wong's hair or DNA on either the containers or in the trunk.

Now Charles had a valid excuse to visit Wu at his warehouse: he needed to secure DNA and hair samples from Wu for comparison.

At least the hair found in the rental car trunk did not match Mike's. Although Mike's fingerprints were on the VdP Vino containers, that fact was expected.

Now Charles had to determine what the plastic and rope strands represented and whose fingers matched the other sets of prints on the containers and the belt.

Charles placed a call to Mike to let him know that so far, nothing in the rental car linked Mike to Wong's murder.

"I was just going to call you, Charles," said Mike with relief. "Thank heavens for small favors regarding the rental car, but the hair and plastic could've been in there a long time. I'm more interested to see whose prints are on my containers."

"I'm with you, Mike," replied Charles. "I do have more very good news for you. According to Olivia, those cats of hers led her to your office in the Knightly tack room, and they found your training calendar. Andrew Knightly will attest that your entry is valid, that you were at the ranch from around 12:30-5:30pm on October 3rd and that the entry has not been tampered with."

"A huge relief," cried Mike. "I forgot completely about the calendar. Of course, I was at the ranch, and I told several people that after Wong's murder, but since I hadn't seen anyone else around that afternoon, I figured I had no way to prove I was there. I'm glad I'm consistent with my training documentation. I was out there today, as well, made my work entry on the calendar and didn't even think about the entry on the 3rd. I'll have to give those cats – and Olivia – a big thank you."

"I'm certain they'll all appreciate that," chuckled Charles.

"Now," questioned Mike with concern, "how are we going to determine whose prints are on the containers, besides mine, since they apparently aren't a match for anyone in your databases?"

Charles decided to tell Mike about his meeting with Chen Wu that morning. "I interviewed Chen Wu earlier, but we did not take any of his DNA as he voluntarily stopped by. I'm going to see if I can find him and make that very request. It was odd Wu wasn't forthcoming about this wine cellar warehouse space of his, but we do know he has a definite interest and a stake in your VdP containers. He also knew Sun Wong previously, with a shady history at that. There's enough suspicion in my mind that I need to follow up and obtain his DNA and prints."

"Well, that won't be difficult," said Mike. "I'm meeting Wu at that warehouse in a half hour to discuss the future of our partnership, and of course, the whereabouts of those containers of mine are the focal point in our current business relationship."

CATAPULT

"Now Mike," warned Charles, "I want you to be careful. We don't know much about Wu – and I gather neither do you – and his behavior has been odd. Added to the Japanese men's testimony that Sun Wong was not happy with finding Wu in Oregon, his history with Wong, and the unusual nickname he seems to have carried with him from Japan – "Scarecrow" – he's just enough out of balance in my mind to make him the prime suspect in this case. I'll be driving over to the warehouse shortly, so I'll meet you there."

"OK, Charles," said Mike. "I've asked Wu to bring the containers I loaned him. I'm going to see if there are any missing."

"Again," warned Charles as he prepared to end their call, "be careful. I'll be along as soon as I can get free here."

Both men sat thinking after the call.

I'm so relieved those cats nudged Olivia's interest to my calendar, thought Mike. *She's smarter than I am. Hell, the cats are smarter than I am. Now I just need to collect my containers and terminate this relationship with Wu. I'll find another investor, but Wu's wiliness borders on dishonesty, and if for no other reason, I don't want to be associated with him in any way*. Mike straightened his desk and put aside thoughts of Olivia and the cats in preparation for the meeting with Chen Wu.

Charles busied himself clearing his desk, as well, but stopped for a moment to consider all that had happened since Sun Wong's murder. *It's all too bizarre*, Charles thought. *The staging at the pumpkin patch that revolved around a catapult and a human scarecrow; Mike's involvement with Chen Wu, his secrecy regarding his VdP Vino investor and his disappearance on the day of the murder; Chen Wu's involvement with Sun Wong, the stock fraud scandal and Wu's disappearance, not to mention earning the name "Scarecrow" known among the Japanese stockbrokers; finding Mike's VdP Vino containers at the murder scene.*

How does this all add up? Has Wu so intricately woven himself into the fabric of Mike's project that Mike can't extricate himself from Wu's control? What part did Wu really play in Sun Wong's death?

Both men hoped to answer their questions, and that this investigation would soon be over.

CATAPULT

CHAPTER 34 -

One reason we admire cats is for their proficiency in one-upmanship. They always seem to come out on top, no matter what they are doing, or pretend they do. Rarely do you see a cat discomfited. They have no conscience, and they never regret. Maybe we secretly envy them. *Barbara Webster* from <u>Creatures and Contentments</u>

Mike Middleton was a man of his word. Although he had serious misgivings about this meeting with Chen Wu, he would confront Wu and sever all ties with the man.

Almost as an afterthought, Mike stuffed his tiny digital recorder in his shirt pocket, grabbed his jacket and began the short journey to the warehouse.

Upon arrival at Chen's wine storage warehouse, Mike noted there were no cars parked in the lot adjacent to the warehouse. Maybe Wu isn't here yet, Mike thought.

Testing the door to the wine cellar area, Mike found that it was unlocked, so he opened it carefully and leaned in.

"Is anyone here?" Mike called. He looked around the darkened room and listened for sounds of life.

Not hearing or seeing anyone, Mike flipped on the lights.

Wu was standing beside a large wine barrel with a gun in his hand.

"Now Chen," Mike began, "you don't want to pose that kind of threat, not when Charles Beltz is right behind me."

"I don't believe you," Wu answered waving the gun and motioning for Mike to step fully inside the door. "I've already spoken with Charles and he seemed quite satisfied with my alibi for Wong's murder. I've been a patient man, my dear partner, but I will only tolerate so much. Wong threatened to expose my past somewhat-dubious business dealings in the Japanese stock market. Your last threat to 'take your product elsewhere' was the last straw for you. It so happens I have a contract for VdP Vino distribution that is very favorable to me. And it contains a near-perfect likeness of your signature affixed to its bottom line. When you're out of the picture, the project belongs to me."

"Now, you know you'll never get away with that, Wu." Mike spoke softly in a conciliatory voice so as not to spook Wu any

further. He needed to stall Wu until Charles
could get there.

"Ha!" cried Wu. "It seems your
usefulness, like that of Sun Wong's, has passed
its expiration date. Move over to this corner
behind me. It's a shame I couldn't have
surprised you like I surprised Wong here. He
didn't have a chance to argue or put up a fight.
Much cleaner that way."

Even though Mike followed Wu's
command, it was necessary to move closer to
Wu to get to that corner. Mike moved slowly,
and as he passed Wu, Mike suddenly lunged for
the gun.

Wu fired but succeeded in inflicting only
a flesh wound to Mike's left arm. By that time,
Mike had wrestled Wu to the floor, outweighing
the slight Japanese man by a good fifty pounds.
Mike shoved the gun out of Wu's reach and he
sat on Wu's chest, pinning Wu's arms to the
floor.

At that moment, Charles burst through
the front door.

"Mike!" Charles yelled pointing his own
gun at the incapacitated Wu. "Are you alright? I
heard a gunshot!"

"He got me in the arm, but it's barely a
scratch, Charles," shouted Mike as Wu
continued to struggle beneath him. "Come get
this guy away from me before I bash his head
in. Seems he was going to kill me — and he
confessed to killing Sun Wong." Mike's grin

broadened. "I just happen to have a recorder operating in my pocket."

"You just saved me a lot of time, Mike," retorted Charles, "but I do wish you'd waited for me so I could do my job. I have a feeling the DNA and prints I'm going to collect from Wu will match that found on your VdP containers. That, added to your recording, should give us what we need to lock Wu up until the Grand Jury can meet."

Charles relieved Mike of his prisoner, cuffed him and called for backup and crime scene techs. He'd seen only one car, Mike's jeep, in the parking lot, so he assumed Wu must have parked blocks away to avoid detection. Charles notified the department to send a deputy to impound that car, too, just in case it might contain something else to incriminate Wu.

"Do you want me to call an ambulance, Mike?" asked Charles, noting a fair amount of blood on Mike's sleeve.

"No, but I'd appreciate if you'd take me to the ER to get it checked," said Mike. "You know anytime a guy presents at the hospital with a GSW, they're mandated to call the police anyway. Having served some jail time, they'll just call your department to arrest me, I fear."

"Sure enough," said Charles. "I've got Wu secured and have given him his rights. My backup is just arriving in the parking lot now. As soon as I can turn him over to them, we'll head to the ER and I'll sign the necessary papers to get you treated."

"Thanks, Charles," sighed Mike. "You know, that will save everyone a lot of time, as the first thing that mandated report would do is land me in jail – again. I think the recorder will establish I was shot defending myself, that I carried no weapon, and that Wu tried to kill me."

"Although it's up to the Grand Jury to indict Wu, we're going to charge Wu with your attempted murder as well as the murder of Sun Wong," said Charles.

"Hey, guys, over here!" Charles yelled to the arriving deputies and CSIs. "Got a present for you, and I believe Mr. Middleton has a recording you can take with you. The suspect has been advised of his rights. You CSIs now have possession of the scene. Mike, let's get you to the hospital. I'm glad to say this episode appears to be coming to an end."

CATAPULT

CHAPTER 35 -

The cat could very well be man's best friend but would never stoop to admitting it. *Doug Larson*

Mike was treated and released from the hospital, thanks to Charles' accompanying him to the ER and completing all necessary paperwork.

Wu was required to submit to DNA testing at the police station, and those specimens along with hair strands were rushed to the lab where the techs were waiting to make the comparison.

Word of Wu's arrest spread like wildfire, in part because Charles called James to let him know his brother was wounded but uncritically, and in great part because James called Mary and Olivia to let them know Mike was alright.

CATAPULT

The cats, of course, including Mona, Mac and Murphy, were apprised of the situation immediately by their humans. George King was called by the department not only as a county commissioner, but also to document the event as editor of the *Jory Hills Times*.

Kate, hearing the news from Charles while at the shelter with Mo, Victoria and Phillip, exclaimed to the cats, "Mike's been wounded! But he's ok and Chen Wu has been arrested in the shooting! Mary is on her way here, as is James with Arbor and Syrah."

At that moment, Kate's cell phone registered a call from Olivia. The two commiserated regarding the entire series of events, each offering thanks that Mike was not seriously wounded. Kate told Olivia that George King was headed to the McMinnville PD to interview Charles for the news story and that James, on his way to the shelter, had been advised that his brother was going to be just fine.

After a 10-minute conversation with Kate, Olivia loaded Lady, Señor, Winston and Squeaker in her car, and started the brief trek to Cats Pause.

Gathered with their respective humans at Cats Pause, the nine cats had already been certain from their sleuthing that Wu had killed Wong. But they were distressed that Mike had been injured in the process of capturing Wu. They were also confident that Mike's alibi, and

Mike's recording of the actual event at the warehouse that morning – were sufficient evidence to exonerate Mike from any involvement while they awaited further lab results.

The lab techs hand-delivered the results of their DNA testing that afternoon.

The second set of fingerprints on the VdP Vino containers matched Wu's conclusively.

The plastic and rope fibers from the rental car trunk were matched with remnants located in the warehouse. Rope and plastic fibers had also been collected at the pumpkin patch, and the samples found in all three locations were verified as the same by the lab.

Hair strands found in the warehouse belonged to Sun Wong and Chen Wu. Since Wong had only arrived on the day of his murder, and had not previously visited the warehouse, the finding of those strands placed him there before he died on that same date.

The McMinnville PD had an airtight case.

George King's story in the *Jory Hills Times* would be published that evening:

Chen Wu, 49, was arrested today at a local warehouse in conjunction with a shooting at the warehouse.

CATAPULT

Michael Middleton, 30, suffered a gunshot wound to his left arm, but was treated at the local hospital and released. Middleton had been unarmed.

Wu's statement alleged that he shot Middleton in self-defense, but a recording of the event does not support that allegation.

In a related incident, Sun Yuen Wong, also 49, of Tokyo, Japan, was killed in Seven Oaks on October 3rd. The cause of death as reported by the medical examiner, was strangulation.

A search of the warehouse where Middleton was wounded revealed evidence that Wong was killed at the warehouse. It was determined previously that Wong's body was moved to a field in Yamhill County after he was killed. His body was discovered in that field on the evening of October 3rd.

Police are holding Wu in the Wong case, and in Middleton's assault.

The Grand Jury will meet tomorrow to hear both cases.

Lt. Charles Beltz of the McMinnville Police Department, advises that charges are pending for attempted murder (of Middleton) and aggravated murder (of Wong).

Later that evening, Charles and Kate, James and Mary, Olivia and Mike, and George King met for dinner. As they discussed the case, they recognized it was currently in the hands of the Grand Jury. They were all confident, however, that the investigation had provided enough evidence to indict – and convict – Chen Wu.

"I can only speculate why Wu killed Sun Wong and tried to kill Mike," offered Charles to the group. "Because he's such an egotist, I'm convinced Wu thought we'd never make the connections between the scarecrow and the catapult to his own motives with respect to his business dealings in the valley."

"I agree, Charles," said Kate. "It was as though Wu was taunting the community and our police with his charade and the staging at the pumpkin patch. Narcissists are known for their blind self-confidence and beliefs that no one can touch them. They think they can outsmart everyone because they are the ultimate gameplayers."

"So, if I understand what you're alleging," Mike mused, "Wu, as the 'scarecrow' overseeing his domain, was using me to 'catapult' himself to secure a monopoly on the VdP Vino market. He'd scare off the competition and he'd forged my name on a sole-operator's contract and since it was such a good likeness I doubt anyone would have questioned its legitimacy after I was 'gone.' Once he had the information he needed, I was no longer useful, and I had to go."

"Correct," replied Charles. "And Sun Wong must have threatened to expose his past, denying Wu his credibility and therefore putting the brakes on Wu's march to gain that distribution foothold here."

"Therefore," George added, "Mike and Wong were both expendable, and, in fact, needed to be eliminated so that Wu could carry on as a legitimate businessman with his forged contract and with total control over Vaso de Premium Vino distributorship."

"I'm so happy your injuries were minor," sighed Olivia. "I would have missed you terribly, and I know my father would like to see more of you at the ranch. He wants to speak with you tomorrow about the horses and the great job you've been doing with their training needs."

"And I'm happy to hear you'd miss me, Olivia," Mike said with a grin. "Looks like it took an injury, though, to get you to have dinner with me."

"Mike," admonished Olivia laughing and blushing at the same time, "during our friendship you never asked me for dinner before tonight! I would've said yes in a heartbeat."

"Well, I can see it's been a very productive day, and now evening," George offered with a hearty laugh. "I, for one, need to leave so I can put the *Jory Hills Times* to bed, so to speak. And I know those cats have found numerous ways to make their presence known at the house. I'll be picking up their trails until midnight."

The group laughed in unison and Charles quickly picked up the check. "You have all been immensely helpful to me, and I hope you'll let me treat you to dinner as a thank-you gesture."

"You don't need to do that, Charles," offered James. "We are your friends and we want to keep you around so our community remains in tip-top shape. We owe you a debt of gratitude for your relentless pursuit of justice in Seven Oaks and our extended community."

The group agreed and as one, shook hands and hugged before heading out to their respective homes.

Where 12 anxious cats impatiently awaited their return.

CATAPULT

CHAPTER 36 -

It is just like man's vanity and impertinence to call an animal dumb because it is dumb to his dull perceptions.
Mark Twain

I just can't believe it's all over but the shouting, meowed Mo. *And I must say that, even with my curiosity peaked above the Alps, I am so glad we were nowhere near that warehouse when the shooting started!*

I agree! squeaked Georgia as the two cats sat greeting newcomers from the counter at the shelter. *There are some things we just should leave to law enforcement. In this case though, Charles must have been shocked when Wu wounded Mike. If he'd only gotten there 30 seconds earlier...*

Or if Mike had waited to enter the warehouse until Charles arrived, countered Mo. *I don't like to think what might have happened if Wu had gotten the upper hand in that combat. Mike is lucky he's a lot bigger than Wu, but he's not trained to take down an attacker like Charles is.*

"Listen to these two," Kate said to Olivia as they, too, greeted guests at Cats Pause. "You'd think they had some kind of inroad to the events of yesterday."

"And well they may, Kate," replied Olivia. "You know they are always present when we're on the phone or when we visit each other – and they're the first ones in the car when there's any kind of excitement in the air. I think they just know…"

"You could be right," laughed Kate as she looked Mo in the eyes. At that moment, Mo chose to look over Kate's head at an imaginary bug on the wall. "Look at her. It's like she knows I'm looking at her and wants me to know she could care less."

"I'm so excited to start work at James' Cats Meow," exclaimed Olivia. "He's going to stop by here today and take me to the clinic to get acquainted with the procedures there. He wants me to start on Monday. I'd like to start today! The cats have permission to accompany me to the clinic whenever they want. They will love visiting with Arbor and Syrah and hopefully they'll also help calm some of the patients. Poor kitties get so scared at the vet's!"

"Have you told your father yet?" asked Kate. "I know you have mentioned in the past that you'd love to be a part of the clinic, but does he know you'll be absent from the ranch most days?"

"I've hinted as much, but I'll go back to the ranch and talk to him again after my indoctrination at the clinic," said Olivia. "I should think he'll be happy for me. Besides, he mentioned that he was going to offer Mike a permanent position as trainer for our horses. So, it's not as though the ranch will be devoid of humans on a day-to-day basis. And I'll be around weekends. Mary would like to help James on weekends, and she will continue helping James with emergencies, so I won't be on call 24/7."

I think Olivia will make a swell veterinary's technician, purred Georgia. *She has a soothing voice, loves cats and look how she handles those giant horses! They treat her with respect as do Winton, Squeaker, Lady and Señor.*

I think James is lucky to have Olivia and Mary, said Mo as she curled up on the counter. *And that puts Mike a bit closer to Olivia, now doesn't it? I like the sound of that.*

Mo

I think I'll take a little snooze, replied Georgia. *All this excitement has worn me out.*

Georgia

Both cats laid down and fell asleep. Well, they never really slept: each had one eye open so as not to miss a thing.

At that moment at the Knightly ranch, Andrew was pouring a cup of very strong coffee for Mike Middleton. He hoped to make Mike comfortable, and was also hoping that Mike would say 'yes' to his offer.

"Well, Mike," he said, "how's that arm? I see some bandages but no blood. Are you sure you were wounded?"

Mike laughed and drank his very black coffee. "Yes, I'm sure. I suppose it must've seemed reckless, and it probably was a bit, but I just couldn't wait for Charles to arrive at the warehouse. And who would imagine that Wu would actually have a gun? He did mention that if he'd been able to surprise me, "it" would've been much easier for him."

"I assume "it" means your murder," shuddered Andrew. "No, a gun just doesn't seem to fit his M.O."

"Glad he's where he should be," allowed Mike, "and I have an appointment with the five Japanese salesmen this afternoon. They are considering sponsoring my VdP Vino project, at least in the beginning, to include service aboard Japan Airlines. That would be a great relief. Once VdP Vino gets off the ground, I should be able to run the operation on my own with no need for more investors."

CATAPULT

"That's wonderful, Mike," exclaimed Andrew. "And, well, it fits in with a proposition I have for you. How would you like to become the permanent salaried trainer at the Knightly Ranch? Now, don't answer just yet. I have a few perks to throw your way, and not just medical insurance, which, from your recent encounter, it appears you can use.

"I have a large back room in the barn, big enough to serve as a small warehouse and workroom. I would offer it to you, rent-free, and you could run your VdP Vino business from here. So, you could have the horses and the single-serving container business all under one roof. I'll cover the entire operation with my insurance. How does that sound?"

"Wow," said Mike, "that's just music to my ears. You know how I love those horses, and I hadn't even gotten around to planning space for my business. That sounds just perfect. Thank you so much, Andrew, and by the way, I accept!"

"Excellent," cried Andrew. "Let's toast the occasion with another cup of my excellent albeit strong coffee. I'm hoping you can begin next week. I know you still have some things to work out with the VdP project."

"It's the best news I've had in a long while, Andrew," said Mike, "and I hope I live up to your expectations."

"You already have, son," replied Andrew. "Just keep doing what you're doing, and you, me, the horses and your containers will go a long way."

As Mike mulled over his good fortune, other than the gunshot wound of course, he couldn't believe things were finally looking up. He so loved the horses at Knightly Ranch and they loved him, too. And then Andrew offered him free office space for his VdP Vino distribution project! He would be closer to Olivia at the ranch, and he'd have more time to dote on those darned cats. They just got to him, and in a good way. It seemed they were always thinking. And they kept the barn and stalls in pristine rodent-free condition.

As he pulled into the alley behind Kat's English B&B, he took time to check his teeth in the mirror and to run a comb through his hair. He didn't want to look like a vagrant when he met with the Japanese businessmen.

Kate was busying herself in the kitchen when he politely knocked at the back door. It was getting on to Tea Time, and he hoped Kate would share some of the luscious scones with a guest of her guests.

"Hello, Mike," exclaimed Kate as she hugged him fiercely. "I'm so happy to see you up and around and with color in your face. I'll tell you, when I heard what happened to you, all the color left mine!"

"I'm almost as good as new, Kate," laughed Mike. "I've just come from Andrew

Knightly's Ranch, and he's not only offered me a job, but is allowing me to use a huge amount of space for my warehouse and distribution of the VdP Vino project. I can hardly believe I deserve such kindness."

"You deserve all that and more," replied Kate as she handed Mike two large scones with cream and blueberries. "And I hope these will make you feel not just *almost* better, but all the way better."

The two entered the dining room where the five Japanese men were sitting at the table and talking in Japanese. Kate, with Mike's help, carried large trays of crustless sandwiches, scones, jam, fruit, cream and several hot teas.

"Oh gee," groaned Mike. "I forgot to bring a translator. How will I pitch my project?"

Just then, George King entered the room. The Japanese men had called George and asked him to be present when they met with Mike.

Kate offered George tea and biscuits, to which he exclaimed, "I was hoping you'd ask! You, too, Mike? We are very lucky, at least in our timing, today."

Kate returned to the kitchen and Mike and George were seated at the dining room table. George had obviously been coached by the Japanese ahead of time because he turned to Mike and said, "These gentlemen unanimously request to invest in your project on behalf of Chan Distributors. They have discussed this with their home office, and all agree. They believe your VdP Vino project has tremendous potential in Japan. Why, with the Japanese wine market still in its infancy, many Japanese are hoping to try as many high-end varieties as possible. The single-serving concept of premium wines is just what the market is begging for. They think you will become a worldwide sensation!"

"Whoa," Mike laughed as he raised his hands in half-hearted objection. "I'm a one-man operation at this point. What I really need is an investor to help me launch the project. I appreciate that the Japanese want many premium wines, but first we have to test the market to see which varieties are most in demand by single serving."

Quan, the man who spoke the most English, appeared to have understood most of what Mike said. He nodded his head in agreement and translated, with George's help, to the other four men.

George took his time, listening, to fully understand the offer to Mike. When the room became quiet, the six men turned toward Mike.

"Mike," began George, "Chan Distributors agrees with your philosophy and your project initiation. They will sponsor your start-up, and, if you agree, you will receive a faxed contract from Chan which you should share with an attorney.

"Chan would like you to run a test market on the wines here – and in Tokyo," continued George, "and you will have the freedom to choose any wines and any wineries you may wish to fill your containers. They also wish you to know that by signing this contract, you are in no way restricted from distribution of your VdP Vino wines anywhere else in the world. They wish to make clear that Chan Distributors and the Japanese wine market are looking for new and innovative ideas, which yours obviously is, but they are not interested in creating a monopoly on distribution nor in restricting your choice of wines."

"I'm very pleased to hear that. Will there be a timeframe for my test market?" asked Mike. "And when would Chan like to receive my written proposal, including estimated start-up costs?"

George spoke with the Japanese men and listened while they discussed the details.

"Mike," continued George, "they ask that you set the timeframe for the actual test, and wait until you've chosen the wines and population of the test market to submit the entire start-up cost delivery. They will make provisions for distribution in Japan, and you will need to work out your other distribution channels separately from this contract, of course. However, they will need to know as soon as possible how much you anticipate will be the cost of the test marketing drive. They'd like to give you what you estimate to need so that you can run with the test, without having to wait for invoices, start-up cost factors, etc."

"It all sounds great," said Mike shaking his head. "I'm so glad you remained in Oregon to speak with me. I'm so sorry for the circumstances and for the loss of Sun Yuen Wong, and I know it hasn't been easy to remain here this long when you have very pressing matters at home."

George translated Mike's agreement and regrets, and they all stood and shook hands. Mike and George bowed in Japanese tradition, and the Japanese were delighted by the gesture.

"One other thing, Mike," said George. "Since they consider you part of the Chan Family, they want you to know they have signed contracts with Kats Jory Hills Estate Winery, Sol Lina/Jackson Wineries, Red Rim and Glory Days wineries to enter the Japanese mass retail market. Most of the wines they will distribute will be Pinot Noirs, but they will also include a variety of Pinot Gris, Chardonnay and a Claret or two. They think it is important for you to know what wines they are distributing in bulk so that you can make informed decisions about the single-serving wine varieties.

"They also want you to know that the Japanese Prime Minister, Shinzo Abe, will be visiting Chan Distributors next month. It is something he rarely does, but they're hoping to have some of your Vaso de Premium Vino product, even if it is in the test batch, to share with him. Apparently, he is a huge wine aficionado. And if you'd honor them further, they will fly you to Tokyo to meet the PM."

"I'm so grateful for the faith they've shown in me," responded Mike with sincerity. "I will work day and night to make the VdP Vino project a success, along with the finest single serving selection for the Japanese market. I'll be sure to include some of the best Pinot Noirs from the valley in the testing. I can ship some samples to Chan early next month to share with the Japanese PM or I can bring those myself, as I'm honored to accept their kind invitation."

They all bowed once more, and Mike and George walked to the kitchen in search of Kate.

"Well, Kate," thundered George. "We just made a deal and new friends in the span of an hour. You know, wheeling and dealing makes me hungry. Have you any leftover scones?"

They all laughed and proceeded to discuss the event of the afternoon.

Unseen under the table, three cats smiled and purred with satisfaction.

CATAPULT

CHAPTER 37 -

Of all the animals, he alone attains to the Contemplative Life. Andrew Lang

Seven Oaks was fairly bustling with as much bustle as can be brought forth in a small town. The cats were gathering at Cats Pause Feline Shelter to gossip and greet visitors. Mo, Phillip and Victoria were waiting impatiently, tails lashing. They couldn't wait to share their respective takes on the events of the past few days.

Olivia stopped by the shelter to tell James that her father soundly approved of her new position at The Cats Meow. Although she'd have less time with the horses, Mike would manage quite well. After all, she lived at the ranch and would still be available to her father whenever he needed her. She couldn't help but mention that she'd see Mike in the afternoons at the ranch because her work at the clinic would end at 4. She had in tow four cats who were delighted to be on a walk-about to the shelter, where they knew most, if not all, of their friends would gather today.

James had stopped by to tell Kate about Olivia's acceptance of the position at the clinic. He, too, was escorted by two cats.

"Now Kate, don't look so sad," said James. "After all, Olivia will still be volunteering here at the shelter. That was an explicit proviso of her contract, that she could not divorce herself of her duties here. She loves all the cats, and her chief concern is that you have enough help here."

"I certainly don't want Olivia to think that she must neglect duties at the clinic to volunteer at the shelter," Kate replied. "I'll try my best to keep her schedule here flexible. Although we need her and she is so good with the cats, she'll be working with cats at the clinic who will need her even more. And she'll be learning such valuable lessons. You are a very lucky man, James."

"You can say that again," laughed James. "I wasn't surprised when Mary started intimating she'd like to curtail her duties at the clinic because she has so many other irons in the fire, including helping you at the B&B and volunteering here at the shelter. She just didn't want to stretch herself too thin. Besides, I think maybe after we were formally engaged, she thought it might be 'overkill' to work together all day and spend evenings together as well. She most certainly wants to be on-call for emergencies, and loves coming to the clinic on weekends. I think she's got a good handle on her time management."

"I guess I'm sort of on the fence about too much of a good thing when it comes to relationships" offered Kate. "I feel I don't see nearly enough of Charles, but then we don't work together. Can you imagine me trying to keep up with him at the McMinnville PD? At one point, I was going to enroll in the Community Contact Program, which allows civilians to help with data entry and organizing at the department, encourages ride-alongs with officers on duty, and provides police science education with accreditation for those who wish the credit for a degree. I went on one ride-along – and that was enough. I'm afraid I'm not cut out for police work. I love my B&B and Cats Pause, and need to spend most of my time with those two jobs. On the other hand, if Charles asked for my help at the department in any capacity, I'd gladly acquiesce. I just wouldn't want to be around the department fulltime."

"That's sort of where Mary is right now," said James. "She says that if we work together all day, we won't have new things to share at night. And she knows I need a fulltime technician at the clinic. I can see it both ways, and whatever makes Mary happy, makes me happy."

As James was leaving the shelter for an appointment at the clinic, George King pulled up to the door and released his three charges, who knew exactly where to go. Mona, Mac and Murphy sprinted to the open door and squeezed between James' legs.

"Such a rush!" exclaimed James. "You'd think there was some kind of meeting of the minds brewing in that shelter. Don't worry, I've left Arbor and Syrah here for a while so they can visit."

"I'm glad I'm not the only one who believes those cats know where they are and what's going on," said George as he climbed out of his van and ambled to the door. "I never cease to be amazed that they know exactly where we are at any given time, and that once they get to where they need to go, I'm dismissed like so much spoiled milk."

The two men laughed at that visual and at the sight of the cats assembling in the shelter greeting room.

"I guess I've served my usefulness today," said George with tears in his eyes from the boisterous laughter he shared with James. "How you work with these little vixens day after day, I don't know. They just lead us around by our noses."

CATAPULT

"Not so much at the clinic," said James still gasping from laughing. "The cats that arrive there are usually terrified. Cats just freeze when they're at the vet's. Probably the smell. We do all we can to calm them and make them comfortable, but especially if they're injured or sick, I can smell the fear. I just know that I'm going to do my damnedest to fix them up, and eventually, they sense that, too."

"You're wonderful with those cats, James," said George, finally recovered from his fit of laughter. "My three don't like getting their shots or their dental exams so they squirm all over the van when they're scheduled for those, but any other time I bring them by the clinic, they seem just fine. What can I say? Cats are smarter than most humans, if you ask me."

"I'll second that," chuckled James. "Good to see you, George. I need to mosey back to the clinic to tend to a very sore foot. I hope Kendall Goodman hasn't been letting her cat wander near those woods. Last year we found traps set by some idiot. In this day and age! Can you imagine? Sometimes I just can't believe some humans' shameful disregard for wildlife, or any life. Don't get me started. I'm glad you're not a hunter, George."

The two parted ways as the cats were doing their strange yet rhythmic circle dance in the lobby.

CATAPULT

Georgia appeared from the back of the shelter, along with Rebecca who had Lawrence Junior on her heels.

There you are, meowed Mo. *We were just getting ready to set off a howl. That always gets Kate's attention. I overheard her say that Rebecca was bringing Junior to the shelter today, but that was an hour ago. Where have you been?*

You wouldn't believe the racket that little Junior can make in the morning, said Georgia. *You'd think someone was putting his eye out. The little guy just screams his head off. He wasn't feeling well the last few days, so he's been bored and we've gone nowhere. Once Rebecca got some food and milk in him this morning, he settled down and took a nap. I tried very hard to be quiet all the way over here because I was afraid if he awoke in another snit Rebecca would turn around and go home.*

Oh, I'm sorry he's been sick. We know you love the little guy, said Lady, *but it must be difficult working around his schedule.*

For me and for Rebecca, replied Georgia. *But we made it and I'm ready for the news. I've been dying to hear what happened as Rebecca has pretty much been housebound the last few days with Junior — and me.*

Thirteen cats can make a lot of noise. Missing only Diana and Edward, who were with their people, the Kensingtons, on a now-extended vacation, the thirteen present at Cats Pause meowed, hissed, spat, growled and gargled endlessly. And since they hadn't been all together in some time, they did so with reckless abandon, oblivious to the stares and giggles from the visitors at Cats Pause Feline Shelter.

Can you believe we're here together? asked Winston. *It's been ages and I'm so happy our humans stay in touch — and that they understand that WE like to stay in touch, too.*

Most definitely! meowed Señor. *Can you imagine if we'd been adopted by people who live in different towns or who weren't such good friends? We'd never see each other, and then how would Seven Oaks ever find its criminals, at least find them in record time?*

I'm sorry that the Kensingtons decided to extend their vacation, sighed Squeaker. *If not for that, we'd ALL be together. I do so miss lovely Diana and handsome Edward.*

I'm sure Diana and Edward are having the times of their lives, offered Georgia. *I don't understand their penchant for travel because I don't particularly care to go beyond Seven Oaks, but those two love it and are practically inseparable from Pippa and Beatrice. I am sorry, though, that they missed helping us solve this crime!*

Well, for certain, Chen Wu will get what he deserves, huffed Lady. *What a sadistic, horrible human. He kills Sun Yuen Wong and* then stuffs him in a plastic bag, takes him to the pumpkin patch, dresses him as a scarecrow – and places him next to the catapult! Then he tries to kill Mike!

I think God gets it wrong every now and then, reasoned Mo, *or he makes some people bad so we can see how good the rest of them really are.*

Of course, I've never known an animal to practice such barbarism, replied Mac.

I beg to differ, Mac, said practical mom Mona. *Don't we take delight in playing with our prey before we eat it? Remember that mouse you batted around the house last week?*

That's different, quipped Mac. *And you, momma, are the one who taught me that behavior. You just love to hassle and chase bugs. I'm not sure you even bother eating them?*

Coming to Mona's defense, Murphy pointed out, S*he taught us how to survive, and we do rid the world of nasty rodents and bugs. I don't ever bother birds because she instilled better behavior in us.*

You're right, Mac apologized. *Sorry, momma, I just got caught up in the moment. I'm so glad George is safe and sound and I know the rest of you are grateful your humans are healthy, happy, and ready for the next adventure.*

At that, all 13 cats howled in unison.

At that, all visitors at the shelter noticed their hair standing on end.

CATAPULT

Kate stood in her office talking with George King and Elizabeth Conley. Elizabeth had returned from her vacation that morning and had stopped by to pick up her two feline companions, Phillip and Victoria.

Rebecca Sherlock was busy following little Lawrence Jr. around the shelter as he 'ooh'd' and 'aah'd' over every cat he saw, including the 13 who were already wound up and moving faster than Junior.

James and Olivia had both left, and would meet at the clinic where Olivia's first tutorial would take place. Mary was last seen in the lobby of the shelter as she attempted to herd the 13 cats to one of the visiting rooms. Lack of cooperation by the cats and interference by Junior made the effort appear fruitless and most hilarious to onlookers.

As the friends joined in discussion about the events of the past few days, Charles dropped by the shelter to say 'hello' to Kate and to give her the latest update on Chen Wu.

"The Grand Jury brought back an indictment on several counts this morning, not the least of which was the aggravated murder of Sun Yuen Wong. They also brought charges in the attempted murder of Mike, assault, abuse of corpse, and several other crimes. I don't anticipate a lengthy trial for Wu, and I also predict a swift verdict of guilty on all counts."

"It is so good to have the worst of this behind us," cried Kate. "The Japanese businessmen are on their way to the airport as we speak. They, too, were glad to put the entire week behind them. I assume Sun Wong's body will accompany them to Japan?"

"Yes, the medical examiner released Wong's body late yesterday," replied Charles. "They have made arrangements for Sun Wong's return on the same flight with his friends. Wong's family will be waiting for them in Tokyo."

"Well, at least we had a lovely farewell breakfast this morning," said Kate as she looked around Charles to the lobby where Mary was still trying to round up the cats. "They spoke not one word about the horror of the week nor did we utter Wu's name. They were so ready to go home, but I know they are also grateful to you for finding Sun Wong's killer and closing the last chapter. Apparently, they were also told their presence at the trial would not be required, and that any testimony needed would be obtained by deposition."

"That's correct," said Charles. "We have everything we need to put Wu away. The only grey area is whether Japan may want to extradite Wu at some point in the future to face any charges there related to the stock market fraud. It may be that the Japanese statute of limitations has run on those crimes."

"Charles, enough of crime and grim talk," Kate said with an exaggerated frown. "Let's resume the pleasantness of life in Seven Oaks, Oregon by planning an engagement party for Mary and James. I think we should host it at Kats Jory Hills Estate Winery. How does that sound?"

"Much better than anything else I've heard today," said Charles, "apart from that cacophony of cats' songs I made my way through a few minutes ago. They all seem perfectly thrilled with each other and not afraid to tell the world."

Kate laughed, as did Charles and George as they could all still hear the mighty meowing ringing off the rafters.

"I feel sorry for Mary," said George wiping his eyes. "She hasn't had a minute's peace since I arrived here with my three. And I don't see it getting any better anytime soon. I think a party at the winery sounds just great, and I'm sure James and Mary will be happy to hear about it, too. Now we only need settle on a date, and we can do that with James and Mary tonight at dinner."

"Oh, that's right," said Elizabeth as Rebecca and Junior appeared in the doorway. "Rebecca, are you able to make dinner tonight at Red Hills?"

"I think not tonight," sighed Rebecca, out of breath from chasing Junior. "Lawrence Jr. is just on the mend from his cold, and I hate to leave him with a sitter, even though he's not contagious and seems to be feeling pretty perky. At least he led me on a merry chase here, whew! If I change my mind later, I'll let you know, but I think I'll probably just settle in with him and a cup of tea, and read a book later. Gosh, sometimes I do feel old, but I actually prefer being home with Junior and Georgia when I'm this tired."

"I don't think I'll make it, either" laughed Elizabeth. "Even though I'm a little younger than you, I'm really feeling my age, too. Besides, I'm a bit jet-lagged and a nice cup of tea, a book and a blanket do sound wonderful. I think I can get the cats to curl up on the hassock at my feet."

"Sounds wonderful," laughed Rebecca as well. "My evenings are no longer quiet, but they can be quite peaceful. Just knowing Junior is sleeping in the other room and Georgia is purring next to me is enough for me."

"Then have a wonderful evening with your families, you two," said Charles. "I need to get back to the department and see if anything new has come up in my absence. Wu was denied bail as he's been determined not only a flight risk but a danger to the community. It was nice to see you all, and I'll see you, Kate and George, tonight. You will remind Mary as soon as she corrals the cats?"

"Yes, Charles," said Kate. "And we'll be breaking up the cats' little tête-à-tête here shortly as we all have things to do. It's getting on to Tea Time, and although I only have two couples checking in today, I do want to be ready with afternoon tea should they desire it."

As the humans made their way into the lobby, they could imagine a collective "*AAWWW*" coming from the cats at the approach of their people.

This is it! meowed Phillip. *We'll be whisked off to our respective homes now. Who knows when we'll all be together again?*

Next time we must make certain that Diana and Edward are present, squealed Arbor. *I do hope they've enjoyed their vacations with the Kensingtons. Pippa and Beatrice are just swell girls.*

Edward

CATAPULT

Diana

Yes, they are and I know Diana and Edward just love them to pieces and the girls don't like to take vacations without their cats. James will pick up Arbor and I in an hour or so, squeaked Syrah, *so we'll have a bit of time to visit with the new arrivals here at the shelter.*

One-by-one the cats left the shelter. Some rode on their humans' shoulders, some followed dutifully their human to his or her respective car, and some streaked ahead to their car to await impatiently the approach of the driver.

Another day in Seven Oaks was coming to an end. Thanks to the thirteen shelter cats, all was right in that little corner of the world.

CATAPULT

Mo, resting after a long day sleuthing.

Arbor is depicted herein by *Sambo.*
Syrah is depicted herein by *Betty Boop.*
Diana is depicted herein by *The Boy (!).*
Edward is depicted herein by *Socks.*
Phillip is represented herein by *Murphy* (complete with eyepatch!).

THANK YOU!

Until we meet again…

Mo

More

Mo the Shelter Cat Mysteries

by

Maureen Murphy Williams

MAUREEN
MURPHY
WILLIAMS

CAT MAN
DEUX

A MO THE
SHELTER CAT
MYSTERY

Shrieking and howling in a makeshift cage, Mo arrived unceremoniously with police escort at Cats Pause Feline Shelter. In the quiet wine-country township of Seven Oaks, Oregon, where drama is beating a parking ticket or recovering a tipped glass of Pinot Noir, Mo's 'mum' has been murdered! Suddenly orphaned and facing life as a shelter cat, Mo enlists new-found shelter feline friends, Phillip, Edward and Diana, to help find mum's killer. Mo, though, must keep a secret she feels will bring harm to her new friends, so she teams up with shelter director, Kate Ferguson to uncover who did the dastardly deed. Kate and Mo investigate why a group of California investors is secretly trying to acquire valuable vineyard land. Through links with the community and the local police, they discover the intent of the buy-up is to rezone the farmlands to develop mega-housing, and destroy the delicate ecosystem and wine producing promise of the Jory Hills AVA. A surprise discovery leads them down a path of intrigue and betrayal; by exposing the plot to ruin the land, they expose the murderer.

MAUREEN MURPHY WILLIAMS

CATASTROPHE

A Mo the Shelter Cat Mystery

WINERY
ENTRANCE

Even the baby raccoons appeared huge to the cats as they shrank to the far corners of their temporary apartments at Cats Pause Feline Shelter. The felines' one objective: avoid the invaders' furry little hands that reached between the narrow bars for leftover cat dinner – lest they become part of the raccoons' diet, too. *Mum, save me*! Mo silently pleaded to her human companion Kate, who was at this hour several miles away and sleeping soundly. Good grief, thought Kate as she sat bolt upright in bed, her head spinning, her eyes blurry from sleep. What is going on at the shelter? Mo reserves telepathy-like pleas for dire emergencies, and she is most certainly sending a distress signal. Kate jumped out of bed and began dressing warmly for her trek into the Oregon winter night. Although Kate knew something was terribly amiss from Mo's frantic pleas, she couldn't know that a raccoon invasion had occurred at the shelter – and that a grisly murder had been committed there as well!

CINCO DE MEOW

A MO THE SHELTER CAT MYSTERY

MAUREEN MURPHY WILLIAMS

The Cinco de Mayo Open House at Kats Jory Hills Estate Winery was in full swing. The event heralded the colossal Memorial Day Weekend happenings in Oregon Wine Country. But Kate Ferguson and her father were saddened by the grim death of a beloved horse trainer and friend, Donald Jenkins. Standing in the shadows of the winery tasting room was a stranger few but John Ferguson noticed. The man listened intently as the holiday revelers circulated around him. Little did he or anyone else in the room suspect, Mo and her feline friends were already in hot pursuit of Donald's killer.

Maureen Murphy Williams' cat detective series, *Mo the Shelter Cat Mysteries*, was inspired by the adoption of Morgan, who spent three years in local shelters awaiting her furr-ever home. Maureen's passion for animal welfare and her love of Oregon wine country are paired to bring a new flavour to the cat detective mystery genre. Maureen resides in Portland with Morgan, and three other rescued cats, Mona, Mac and Murphy, portrayed in Seven Oaks as the domesticated feral family of Commissioner George King.

www.ingramcontent.com/pod-product-compliance
Lightning Source LLC
Chambersburg PA
CBHW070557130626
46556CB00001B/188